I0452070

VAN DYNE'S ZUVEMBIES

PIERCE MOSTYN PARANORMAL INVESTIGATIONS
BOOK 7

C W HAWES

CWH BOOKS

For Jack Koblas, who's gone but not forgotten

ENTER THE IMAGINATIVE WORLD OF CW HAWES

Enter my world. A world of terror on a cosmic scale. Just click, tap, or scan the QR code below.

Fear is the most primal of human emotions. And fear of the unknown is the most terrifying of all fears.

If you are new to the Pierce Mostyn Paranormal Investigations series, then *Van Dyne's Zuvembies* is an excellent entry point into the series and into my world.

In addition to my Pierce Mostyn Paranormal Investigations books, I've written short stories set in the world of the macabre and arcane. Many of which are only available to folks on my mailing list.

So just click, tap, or scan the QR code to enter my world of terror and the macabre. You will get a free copy of *The Feeder* and you'll get my monthly email of news and curated contact. Terror awaits!

PROLOGUE

SHE LOOKED AT THE ADDRESS, back at the slip of paper, and then back at the number over the door.

This is the place, she thought, and walked down the short walk to the door. A man, coming out, held the door for her.

"Thank you," she said, and entered the building. An ordinary, nondescript three-story on Northern Boulevard in Queens.

The directory in the lobby told her she wanted the third floor. At the elevator, she pressed the up button and waited. There was a bit of a musty odor to the old and dingy carpet, and the young woman wrinkled her nose at the smell. When the elevator doors opened, she got in, and pressed three. In a moment the doors opened once more, she got out, and turned into the corridor.

Suite 304 was to her left. She walked a dozen steps and stopped in front of a plain door with frosted glass window and the name Asher and Associates painted on the glass in black letters.

She looked once more at the slip of paper, took a deep

breath, and exhaled. Her hand pushed down on the door handle, and giving it a push, the door opened, and the young woman walked in.

There was a small waiting room with a half-dozen beige plastic chairs lined up along one wall. A pretty little redhead, with the most beautiful smile, sat behind a desk opposite the plastic chairs. A counter fronted the desk, and a sign announced that the desk was home to the receptionist.

The redhead, smile still in place, said, "How may I help you?"

"I'm Sofia Rivera. I have an appointment for three."

The receptionist looked at her computer screen, tapped a few keys, and studied the screen for a moment.

Sofia was jealous. How could anyone be so happy as to smile like that?

The redhead looked at her. "Please have a seat. The therapist will be with you in a minute."

Sofia sat and put her hand in her pocket for her phone. It wasn't there, and the anger bubbled up. Why did they have to take her phone away? It was so unfair. And if her sister hadn't blabbed...

God, I hate Maria, she thought. *Why can't Dad take my side? And that woman he married. She really, really has it in for me. I hate them. I hate them all.*

A door next to the receptionist opened, and a dark-skinned Indian woman called her name.

Sofia got up and walked over to her.

The woman smiled and said, "I'm Kashvi Pushpagiri, your therapist. Follow me."

She led Sofia to a room that was on the spacious side, indicated a chair for her to sit in, and took a seat in the chair across from her. A round coffee table sat between the two chairs.

"So tell me why you've come to see me."

"Everyone's against me."

The therapist arched an eyebrow. "Everyone?"

"My dad never takes my side. My sister's a blabbermouth. My step-mom thinks I'm worthless and turns my dad against me. I just hate them."

"You hate them? Actually hate them?"

There was a pause. "Well, maybe *hate* is a little strong."

"Is it? Perhaps you *do* hate them. Didn't they wrong you? Aren't *they* against *you*?"

"Well, yeah, they are."

"Have you considered that perhaps *they* hate *you*?"

"Really?"

Pushpagiri nodded.

"Wow. I never thought of that. I mean, like, I can see my step-mom, and maybe my sister, but my dad?"

"Did you want him to marry your step-mom?"

"Hell, no!" Realizing what she'd said, Sofia, somewhat embarrassed, apologized. "Sorry."

"That's quite all right. You are in emotional pain. Those who should love you, don't. You are all alone. But I'm here to help." Kashvi favored Sofia with a smile.

"You really think they're against me?"

"Why are you defending them?"

"I'm not!"

"Sounds like it to me. Do you want to be walked on your entire life?"

"No. No, I don't want that."

"Your sister blabbed something which you trusted her to keep a secret."

Sofia nodded.

"What was it?"

"I had my boyfriend over when Dad and Lu, that's my step-mom, Lucinda, when they were out."

"And that's a problem?"

"Well, uh, we were, uh, in my room and..."

"You were having sex."

"No, not sex. But we were, well, you know."

"Making out."

"Yeah."

"And your sister told your dad and step-mom and you got in trouble."

"She even called me a slut! Lu did. She should talk."

"Sofia, it's very important, if you want to become a strong woman, it's very important for you to face and express your rage. You must voice your hate. We at Asher and Associates practice what we call primal rage therapy."

"I just want what's fair."

"We all do."

"So what's this primal rage thing?"

"Women have been held down for a long time. Essentially ever since humans began. Prehistoric women, because they were weaker than men, were abused by them. Skeletons of those prehistoric women show what are commonly called abuse fractures. And let's face it: nothing's changed. We are still being abused. Biologically we carry the rage, the hate, of our abuse in our DNA. That's why it is very important for us to let it out. To stop repressing it. We must go back to our primal state and rage against our oppressors."

"How do I do that?"

"By using the oppressors and abusers we face today to take us back to our primal selves. Each day, you must do a five-minute hate. Put the picture of one of your oppressors before you and scream out your hate. Change the picture each day. Did you bring a picture with you?"

Sofia nodded. "I brought a picture of my sister."

"Good. Let's practice the five-minute hate right now. Put the picture on the coffee table. Let's hate her together."

For five minutes Kashvi Pushpagiri and Sofia Rivera hurled abuse and hateful words at the picture. They screamed at it and hit it. When the five minutes were over, Sofia felt exhausted, yet invigorated.

"I'm going to give you our special primal hate drink." Kashvi walked over to a shelf, retrieved a bottle, and gave it to Sofia. "Drink this tonight and while doing so fill your mind with hateful thoughts. Remember how freeing the five-minute hate felt?"

Sofia nodded.

"Think those thoughts again while drinking the contents of this bottle."

"That's it? Just drink this?"

"Yes and don't forget the hateful thoughts while drinking. It doesn't taste very good, so drink it quickly. You have to drink all of it. Thinking the hateful thoughts helps the medicine go down." Kashvi smiled.

Sofia looked at the bottle, and then at her therapist. "Okay."

"That's it. See you next week. Brittany will set you up with an appointment."

Kashvi stood and walked Sofia out to the lobby.

At the door they said goodbye. Kashvi went back to her office and Sofia walked over to the reception desk.

The redhead gave her an appointment card with a date and time on it. "Does that work for you?"

Sofia looked at the card and nodded. "Does this stuff really work?"

The redhead smiled. "Yes, it does. You will be a whole new person."

Sofia smiled and left the office. On the elevator going down, she realized how free she'd felt after that hating. She actually felt good and empowered. And she liked feeling good.

1

BARDON CALLS

SPECIAL AGENT in Charge Pierce Mostyn woke to the screams of Doctor Dotty Kemper. She was sitting in bed next to him, screaming and shaking. He sat up, put his arms around her, and said soothing words to her. The screams stopped, and the shaking subsided. They were replaced with gentle sobs and tears.

"It's not working, Pierce. Every time I let down and try to relax, the nightmares come."

"I know, Dot. I know. After what we've seen, it's a wonder we're sane."

She nodded, and he kissed away her tears.

"Believe me, it will get better."

She looked at him, although the room was dark, and reached out, touching his face. "Will it? Will it get better, Pierce?"

"Yes, it will."

"Will you hold me?"

"Sure, Dot."

She lay back down. He did likewise and held her close to

him. It didn't take long before her breathing softened and he knew she was once again asleep.

How often can you look into the void, Mostyn wondered, *and maintain your sanity when what you see drives everyone else insane?*

He thought of the Russians locking away political prisoners in insane asylums for the sole purpose of driving them mad.

Yet that was nothing compared to creatures so horrible they made your worst nightmare seem like a children's lullaby. That's what they, in the Office of Unidentified Phenomena, dealt with every day. Insanity producing terror day in and day out. What surprised Mostyn was that relatively few OUP personnel actually went insane. That fact was the reason he believed Doctor Bardon was busy working his magic to protect their sanity. If only he could end the nightmares.

Somewhere in his musings, Mostyn fell asleep. What woke him the second time was his phone. He answered it on the third ring.

"Mostyn."

"Ah, Pierce, my boy, sorry to wake you on this beautiful morning, but we have a case the FBI reluctantly brought us in on. It's beginning to look as though it is more in our line than theirs. Come in at your earliest leisure, but do make it this morning. And bring Doctor Kemper with you."

"Yes, sir. See you later."

The phone went silent. And Mostyn once again found himself wondering how Bardon knew who he was sleeping with.

———

Doctor Rafe Bardon, the director of the Office of Unidentified Phenomena, had his office in a nondescript federal office building in Washington, DC. However, his personal office was anything but nondescript. It always reminded Mostyn of something he might find in a nineteenth century British men's club.

Bardon was sitting behind his heavy black walnut desk, smoking an old yacht-shaped briar pipe; the dark brown wood had turned almost black from years of use. The director seemed sublimely ignorant of the no smoking policy in federal buildings and no one thought it wise to inform him.

Mostyn and Dotty Kemper sat across from their boss in identical Westminster Chesterfield dark chocolate brown leather chairs.

"Sorry to disturb you so early, but the FBI is at their wit's end on the case and requested we get up to speed as soon as possible. You'll be working with Special Agents Lucas Washington and Daniel Garcia. Special Agent in Charge William Wang is not at all pleased at having to work with us. And therefore Washington and Garcia may be reserved, even for FBI agents. Of course Wang believes we're a special group within the Intelligence Branch of the FBI. Any questions?

"What are we dealing with, sir?" Mostyn asked.

Bardon pushed a folder across his desk, and Mostyn retrieved it.

"There have been a series of brutal murders. Entire families wiped out, although in each case one family member has gone missing."

"And the murders are all the same?" Dotty asked.

"Yes, and that is what is puzzling our friends at the FBI. How can a family killed in Queens fit the exact same profile as one murdered in Cleveland, and Seattle, and Los Angeles, and Omaha?"

"How did the people die?" Dotty asked.

"It's all in the report, but I'll give you a brief sketch. In Queens, three members of the Rivera family, father, step-mother, and one daughter were found dead. The older daughter, Sofia, is missing.

"In Omaha, the Williams family was killed by the father. Mother and three children. However, daughter Laqueesha is missing."

"How did the step-mother and father in Queens die?"

"That's the key, Doctor Kemper. Mr. Rivera died from a stab wound in his chest which pierced his heart, and the forensic evidence indicates that he was probably attacked in the kitchen. Mrs. Rivera died from a meat cleaver blow that split her head and the daughter was hacked to death by the same cleaver. Mother and daughter dying in their beds."

"And the cleaver was found in Mr. Rivera's hand," Dotty said.

"Very good, Doctor Kemper." Bardon's eyes were twinkling.

Dotty smiled. "So the question is, how? And was Mr. R stabbed first?"

"How, indeed, Doctor Kemper, and, yes, Mr. Rivera was apparently stabbed before the others died at his hand," Bardon said. "The FBI has been focused on finding the missing girl in each of the situations, and in the process is overlooking the obvious."

"Which is?" Mostyn asked.

"In 1938 a story was published in a pulp magazine. It told of a family being wiped out by a creature known as a zuvembie. The story is actually a thinly disguised account of a real event that happened a few years prior to the publication date. Deemed too fantastic for the true crime magazines, the writer submitted the account to a fiction magazine as a story."

"So you're thinking we're dealing with a zuvembie," Mostyn said.

"Not *a* zuvembie, my dear boy. Zuvembies. Plural."

2

ZUVEMBIES

MOSTYN, Special Agents DC Jones and Kymbra NicAskill, and Doctor Carter Heber, a cryptozoologist with the OUP, sat around a table with FBI Special Agents Washington and Garcia. Off to the side sat Special Agent in Charge William Wang.

The OUP personnel listened while Washington and Garcia brought them up to date on the investigations into the related cases.

All told, the FBI was aware of eight separate incidents. All, however, were similar. In each one, a young female member of the family was missing. And in each one, the murder weapon was in the hands of the person who had, most likely, been murdered first.

There was a third anomaly that the FBI was keeping hush-hush. At three of the murder scenes, the FBI had lost personnel.

"What happened?" Mostyn asked.

Special Agent Washington shook his head. "It was the same basic MO. At the Seattle scene, Agent LaToya Carver was found dead with a knife in her chest. Right through her heart. A knife had been used on the family.

"At El Paso, Special Agent Juan Perez had his head caved in with a fireplace poker. A crowbar had been used to kill the family.

"And in Boston, Agent Patrick Ravi was smothered with a plastic bag over his head. Just like the family."

"No firearms?" NicAskill asked.

Agent Garcia nodded. "There was one. Omaha. A three fifty-seven magnum at point blank range."

"Shit," NicAskill muttered.

"Yeah," Garcia replied. "Wasn't pretty."

"So, you guys have any ideas?" Washington asked. "Ever run across something like this?"

Mostyn shook his head. "No. This is a new one."

"We thought you knew something, and that's why you were brought in," Garcia said.

"Wish we did—" Mostyn was cut off by a snort from William Wang. He ignored the FBI man and continued. "However, you've provided us with a lot of valuable intel. Hopefully, we can get to the bottom of this. And soon."

Wang uncrossed his legs. "Yeah, right. I'm willing to bet my retirement that this case gets quietly slipped into an X-File and just disappears."

Mostyn eyed Wang. After a moment he said, "You know as well as I do that the X-Files don't exist."

"And the moon is made of green cheese."

Mostyn looked at all three FBI men, and said, "We're done here for now. Thank you, gentlemen."

Jones was up and held the door for Mostyn, NicAskill, and Heber. They left the FBI building and got into the black unmarked sedan. With Jones behind the wheel, the car joined the DC traffic.

Mostyn, in the front passenger seat, turned his head and looked at the cryptozoologist. "So what do you think?"

"I'll need more evidence, to be sure, but I would say this particular cryptid has all the signs of being a zuvembie."

"Can someone please tell me what the hell a zuvembie is?" NicAskill asked.

Doctor Heber cleared his throat. "A zuvembie is a creature that is often classed as one of the undead."

"You mean like zombies and vampires?" NicAskill asked.

"Yes. Although technically speaking, a zuvembie is not dead. Simply changed." Heber paused a moment to clean his glasses. He put them back on and continued.

"In traditional voodoo, a bokor, that is, a magician, creates a zombie from someone who is already dead. A zombie is a re-animated corpse that does the bidding of the bokor. A zombie is essentially a slave."

"So there's no zombie virus?" Jones asked.

"No. That is the stuff of cheap pulp fiction and B-rated movies."

"So no zombie apocalypse," Jones said.

Heber shook his head. "I'm afraid not."

"So if a zombie is a dead person made into a slave, what's a zuvembie?" NicAskill asked.

"As I said," Heber explained, "a zombie is a slave of the bokor, created by powerful spells that are cast by the bokor. A zuvembie, on the other hand, has never died. The creator of a zuvembie may or may not be a bokor. What is essential is that the creator of the zuvembie has gone through the necessary rituals and been taught the secret of making the Black Brew, which, when drunk, will turn a woman into a zuvembie."

"Only women can become zuvembies?" Jones asked.

"That is correct," Heber replied. "Only women."

"Why?" The question came from NicAskill.

"Because hate and revenge are the motivators and the required emotions to become a zuvembie." Heber shrugged. "It seems women, as a sex, have so often been viewed and treated as inferior that they and they alone possess the necessary hatred and desire for revenge to become a zuvembie."

NicAskill sat back in her seat. "Wow."

Heber, a smile on his face, continued. "For every action there is an equal and opposite reaction. The zuvembie is the personification of female hate and revenge."

"So what's this thing like?" Jones asked.

Heber explained, "According to the lore, ancient lore that predates voodoo and goes back to West African snake religions, once a woman drinks the Black Brew she ceases to be a human. She becomes one with the denizens of the Black World. Friends and family cease to exist for her. A zuvembie has command over some aspects of nature. It can control owls, snakes, bats, and werewolves to do its bidding. The creature can summon darkness in order to blot out a small amount of light.

"Unless killed by lead or steel, it lives forever. Time means nothing to the zuvembie; it exists, as it were, outside of time. It no longer eats human food and dwells in a house or a cave much as a bat does.

"The zuvembie cannot speak, at least not as humans do, and it does not think as humans think. However, by the sound of its voice it can hypnotize the living and summon a person to his or her death. And once the thing has killed a person, it can control the lifeless corpse until the corpse grows cold and the blood ceases to flow. The corpse becomes the slave, as it were, of the zuvembie and will do whatever the zuvembie commands it to do."

"Good night," Jones said. "It's a good thing women don't know about this zuvembie thing."

"Shut up, Jones," NicAskill said.

"One more thing," Doctor Heber began. "The zuvembie has but one pleasure in life."

"What's that?" Mostyn asked.

"To kill human beings."

3

CAPTURED

DOCTOR DOTTY KEMPER, one of the foremost forensic anthropologists in the world, and a long time operative with the OUP, looked at the body of Serena Thomas.

Kemper had insisted on visiting Hoboken, New Jersey first because it was the closest of the murder scenes. In addition, it just so happened to be the first of the eight mass murders. The deaths of Philip and Serena Thomas had occurred twelve weeks ago. Their only daughter, Kelsey, was missing.

Dotty Kemper turned the head of Serena Thomas to get a better look at the wound. In a corner stood an FBI man.

According to the report, her skull, and the skull of her husband, Philip, had been caved in by a marble rolling pin. To Dotty's eye, the wound looked consistent with the type of damage a marble rolling pin would do to a skull when swung with considerable force.

She agreed with the report of the medical examiner: death would have been instantaneous, or nearly so. The evidence indicated Serena had been hit on the head in daughter Kelsey's room. A single blow. The trail of blood led from

Kelsey's bedroom to that of Philip and Serena's. Philip had been hit twice while sleeping in bed. Serena's body was found on the floor next to her husband's side of the bed, rolling pin in her hand. Tests of the physical matter on the rolling pin confirmed that skin, hair, and blood from both Philip and Serena Thomas were present, indicating the rolling pin was the weapon that had killed both of Kelsey's parents.

Kelsey herself had not been seen since the murder. The extended family was questioned, but said they did not know of the girl's whereabouts. The FBI, after a large-scale and detailed surveillance of the extended family, concluded that Kelsey was not with them, and had either been abducted or had fled.

The examinations by Doctor Christopher, the ME, of the Thomases had been exceptionally thorough. Dotty found nothing she could add. She turned the victim's head back to its original position and returned the body to the cooler.

Tomorrow she'd be in Queens. She'd already spoken with the medical examiner in New York. From the way he'd answered her questions, she doubted she'd find anything new. The FBI had made sure the exams were thorough.

———

While Dotty was examining the bodies of Philip and Serena Thomas, Mostyn, Jones, NicAskill, Willie Lee Baker, the team's photographer, Helene Dubreuil, and Doctors Frederica von Dampst and Carter Heber, drove out to the house where the murders had taken place.

The Thomas home was a modest, nondescript two-story, with a living room, dining room, kitchen, and bathroom on the ground floor, and four bedrooms on the second floor. One of the bedrooms had been turned into a TV room, and another into a craft room.

Upon entering, Doctor von Dampst, who was a clairsentient, set the stage. "Oh!" she exclaimed. "Such anger! Such hatred!"

Mostyn encouraged her to go on, but a look of puzzlement had settled on her face.

"I don't feel any death agony," she said. "Death must have come swiftly and it must've been unexpected."

Mostyn nodded, and Doctor Heber said that would be consistent with a zuvembie.

Heber continued, "The creature would have lulled its victim into a hypnotic state, and probably called him or her to itself, and then killed the person. The victim most likely was not aware of what was happening."

After looking over the first floor, Baker taking photos of everything, the team went upstairs.

"The hatred is much stronger here," von Dampst said.

The team members circulated through the rooms, Baker taking lots of pictures. Von Dampst, however, kept coming back to the hallway and looking up at the door to the attic.

"The hate is very strong coming from the attic," von Dampst said.

Mostyn thought a moment, then said, "Let's take a look. Helene, you're on."

Helene Dubreuil looked human, a member of homo sapiens. She was tall, with exceedingly fair skin, and long black hair. There was a certain Native American quality about her facial features. But she wasn't human, at least not a human from this dimension.

She was from the subterranean world of K'n-yan and her people came to this dimension and then on to Earth with the

Great Old Ones untold eons ago. In many ways, she was a superior being when compared with humans from the surface of good old planet Earth.

Helene smiled at Mostyn, and when the door to the attic was opened, and the stairs lowered, Helene dematerialized.

Jones and NicAskill moved their hands to their firearms. For this assignment, their weapons were loaded with lead semi-wadcutters. They wanted to make sure the zuvembie would die if they had to shoot it. Doctor Bardon's preference was to capture one alive for study.

After several long minutes, Helene rematerialized at the foot of the ladder.

"Is she there?" Mostyn asked.

"She is there, Mostyn Pierce, but she is hidden."

"What do you mean?" Jones asked.

"She is underneath the floor."

"How did you find her?" Mostyn asked.

"Doctor von Dampst seemed sure she was in the attic. But I did not see her in the open space between the floor and the roof. So I started to move through the spaces where you cannot go, and that is how I found her."

"You mean under the floor?"

Helene nodded.

Mostyn smiled. "Very clever of you."

"Thank you, Mostyn Pierce."

"But how can she be under the attic floor?" NicAskill asked.

"She has molded herself to fit between the floor boards of the attic and the ceiling of this floor," Helene explained, "and between those other boards. What are they called?"

"The attic joists?" Jones said.

"Yes, that is what they are. She has molded herself to fit

between the joists, the attic floor, and this ceiling above us. It is a small space in which she is hiding."

"Very interesting this bit of information," Doctor Heber said. "This plasticity is something new. We've never encountered it before now."

"How do we get rid of her?" Jones asked.

Doctor Heber's face turned red. "Get rid of her?" he nearly shouted. "We need to capture her for study. That is what Doctor Bardon wants."

Mostyn nodded. "You're right, Doctor Heber, we need to try to capture this thing."

Jones shook his head. "Okay. How?"

"First, we need the earmuffs," Heber explained. "If we cannot hear its voice, then we cannot be hypnotized by it. Then we try to tranquilize it. We don't know if it responds to tranquilizers or not. The body is still physical, although this plasticity is something of which we weren't aware."

"I have an idea," Helene said.

"What is it, Ms. Dubreuil?" Heber asked.

"Prepare the containment box. I will do the rest."

In Mostyn's opinion, the look on Heber's face was one of pure skepticism, and perhaps it was even colored with resentment. "Just do it, Heber," he told the doctor.

"Very well," Heber replied, the tone of his voice indicating grudging consent.

Jones, NicAskill, and Heber retrieved the containment box, earmuffs, and tranquilizer gun from the SUV, and returned to the house.

The containment box was unfolded and set up. Jones loaded the dart into the gun and stood facing the box. Everyone put on their earmuffs.

Helene closed her eyes and reached out towards the attic

with her hands. Then she turned towards the box and within it, sitting on its haunches, appeared the zuvembie.

Hatred contorted and disfigured its face, but the resemblance to the young woman Mostyn had seen in the photographs of Kelsey Thomas was still evident. She was dressed in pajamas. Her hands had transformed into black nailed claws. The thing's mouth was open, but Mostyn heard nothing thanks to the ear protection. Jones aimed and fired the tranquilizer gun. The dart hit the zuvembie square in the chest. In about fifteen seconds it slumped back against the bars, no longer awake.

Mostyn took off his earmuffs. "Let's go, folks, let's get that thing out of here and back to the lab."

Jones leaned over to Heber, and in a stage whisper said, "See, Doc, Helene makes everything easy-peasy."

Heber looked at Helene and wondered if Bardon had made the right call in allowing this extra-dimensional alien to be out and about on planet Earth. She was, after all, essentially a cryptid. Perhaps the source of all those ghost stories, or the pixie and shapeshifter legends. In fact, did anyone actually know what she was fully capable of? He certainly didn't, and he doubted that Bardon did either. After all, she came here with the Great Old Ones, if her story was to be believed.

No, he thought, *she belongs in a lab somewhere, so I can study her. We need to learn just how dangerous she is to us humans.*

4

WHAT'S IN NEW JERSEY?

MOSTYN LOOKED over his team members and FBI special agents Washington and Garcia. The new person at the table was Doctor Roderick Gerstner, a mythologist and folklorist who'd worked with Mostyn on a previous case involving the Van Dyne Corporation. Gerstner was interested in the zuvembie from the folklore angle and had requested to work on the case. Mostyn and Bardon had both agreed he'd be an asset.

"What I want to know," Washington asked, "is how did you find the murderer? We searched that place from top to bottom and inside out."

"And why all of a sudden are we out of the picture?" Garcia asked.

Mostyn thought carefully about his answers. He and his team were supposed to be from the Intelligence Division of the FBI, because less than two or three dozen persons in the entire federal government even knew of the OUP's existence, and fewer still what the agency actually did.

Mostyn shrugged. "I don't know, Special Agent Washington. You tell me."

Washington folded his arms across his chest, disgust written all over his face.

Garcia repeated his partner's question.

Mostyn said, "You've heard of the X-Files?"

"Yeah," Garcia replied, "the files you told Wang don't exist."

"They don't. At least officially."

"Oh, for the love of God," Washington blurted. "Now they're going to hit us with this top secret spook shit, Dan." He turned to face Mostyn. "Are you serious, Mostyn? We have eight murder situations here, with a body count of thirty-five, and you're going to sit there and tell us these people were killed by little green men in flying saucers? Shit."

Jones, with a grin on his face, said, "Actually, they're gray."

"Oh, for... Fuck you, Jones," Washington spat.

Dotty, her face serious and her voice level, said, "He's right. They are gray. I've seen them."

Washington's face showed he wasn't convinced.

Special Agent Daniel Garcia spoke, "So, in other words, you've come across something that is highly classified. Something way above the pay grade of us ordinary schmucks."

"That's one way of putting it," Mostyn replied.

Washington shook his head. "Wang said we wouldn't be happy." He stood and said to Mostyn, "Enjoy." He turned to his partner. "Come on, Dan, we ain't good enough for these folks." And the two men left the room.

When the door had closed, Willie Lee Baker said, "I kind of feel sorry for them. I know I'd hate to have the rug pulled out from under me in the middle of a project."

"Especially with them being FBI agents," NicAskill said. "They're usually the kings of the roost."

"Of course, they don't know that we aren't FBI," Dotty said.

"Would only make it worse if they did," NicAskill added. "At least they think they were pushed aside by their own. That has to ease the pain a bit."

Dotty shrugged. "Maybe. Maybe not."

Jones leaned towards Dotty. "Are they really gray?" he asked.

"If I told you, I'd have to kill you," Dotty said.

Mostyn added, "Need to know, Jones."

NicAskill elbowed him in the ribs. "And you, Jonesy, don't need to know."

"We have two new murders," Mostyn said. "Yesterday."

NicAskill's eyebrows shot up. "Wow. Whoever or whatever is behind this isn't letting up."

"Doesn't look like it," Mostyn replied. "Number nine is right here in basically our backyard. Up in Jersey City a man was found murdered. A hatchet embedded in his head. And in Minneapolis, two women were murdered. Both with a carving knife to the heart. The third roommate is missing."

Doctor Bernard Able, a parapsychologist with the OUP, who looked somewhat like Sigmund Freud, and did his best to accentuate that look, right down to the cigar, said, "Doesn't murder number nine break the pattern?"

Mostyn shook his head. "Sorry, I forgot to add that Mr. Farber, the victim, had a wife, Sandra, and she is missing."

Able nodded. "And the three roommates could have formed a quasi-family structure. Therefore, number ten also fits the pattern."

"Are we going to New Jersey tomorrow?" Dotty asked.

"We are," Mostyn replied. "It's close."

"What puzzles me," Jones said, "is what's the motive behind all the outbreaks of these zuvembies. I mean, they can't all be coincidences. There's just too many of them. Unless there's a zuvembie virus."

Heber shook his head. "No, there is no zuvembie virus."

Agent Carter Ramsey, the drone surveillance expert, who'd been preoccupied with his tablet for the entire meeting, said, "This isn't the movies, Jones. This is real life."

"And what would *you* know about real life? All you do is play video games," Jones shot back.

"All right," Mostyn said, "let's play nice."

"Well, if there's no virus," Jones said, "then how is this Black Brew stuff getting to all these women? I mean somebody has to be giving it to them."

Doctor Bernard Able made something of a show putting on his gold-frame pince-nez and reading a sheet of paper. He then looked at the group. "Is it possible this affliction is somehow being transmitted through hypnosis or telepathy?"

Heber shook his head. "No. Everything indicates this is a normal occurrence of zuvembie activity, except for the sheer number of them becoming active in such a short period of time."

Gerstner nodded his concurrence.

"Yes, but what if it isn't?" Able pressed.

"What are you getting at, Doctor?" Mostyn asked.

"I'm speaking of the difference between voodoo magic and scientific methodology," Able explained.

"Regardless of whether it's magic or science," Mostyn countered, "we still need to find the creator. The person who is making the zuvembies. And we need to discover his or her motive for doing so."

Able persisted. "But knowing how the creation is taking place might give us a clue."

Heber pursed his lips in thought for a moment before speaking. "To our knowledge, zuvembies can only be created by means of the Black Brew. If some sort of scientific methodology is at work, this would be something completely new. Something completely unknown. However, as far as I know, the creation of zuvembies is out of the realm of current scientific knowledge."

Able leaned back in his chair. "How do you account for the sheer number of zuvembies being created? An awful lot of Black Brew would need to be involved, wouldn't it?"

Heber nodded. "It would."

"Is that likely?" Able pressed.

"Not very," Heber conceded.

"Then a scientific answer is possible."

"I suppose it is, Doctor Able," Heber admitted.

"At this point," Mostyn said, "there are too many unknowns. Hopefully our trip to New Jersey will provide us with some answers. Other than the first responders, the site should have no other contamination. Our job will be to look for anything that might tie these cases together and provide us with information as to who is creating these monsters.

"A couple of people are, at this moment, at work sifting through all the evidence the FBI has collected, just in case they missed something."

NicAskill raised her hand, and Mostyn indicated she had the floor. "You know, Boss, the first murder was in New Jersey and now one of the new ones is again in New Jersey. It could be a coincidence, but I don't believe in coincidences. Two murders in New Jersey—"

And before she could complete her sentence, Mostyn finished it for her, "And Van Dyne Corporation is in New Jersey."

At the same time, Dotty, Baker, and Jones all said, "Oh, shit."

5

A CLUE

MOSTYN and his team had driven up to Jersey City from DC the previous night in two big black unmarked SUVs and stayed in a hotel close to J. Owen Grundy Park and the New Jersey waterfront.

For a late supper, the team went to the Zeppelin Hall Biergarten and ate their fill of burgers, sausages, and the giant pretzels imported from Munich. All washed down with liberal amounts of imported German beer.

In the morning, after a quick breakfast at the hotel, the team, except for Dotty, drove to the crime scene, which was located in a five-story, rather narrow, light brown and tan brick apartment building on Mercer Street. Dotty was dropped off at the morgue to examine the body.

The team walked in and took the elevator to the second floor apartment that had once been the home of Ronald and Sandra Farber. The cop on guard duty opened the door in response to seeing their IDs. Once inside, Mostyn turned to Doctor von Dampst.

"Anything?" he asked.

"Yes. I feel the hate," she said. "It is very palpable. This was not a happy couple."

"Why the hell do people stay together if they aren't happy?" NicAskill asked of no one in particular.

"Force of habit," Baker replied.

NicAskill shook her head. "Idiots."

Baker chuckled. "Inertia. The greatest force in the universe."

NicAskill blew a raspberry.

"Check everything," Mostyn said. "We need to find the creature and we need to find the clue that ties all of these cases together."

The team members scoured the apartment. Baker took pictures and Ramsey sent a drone to access the very difficult to reach places. After fifteen minutes, von Dampst informed Mostyn the zuvembie was not in the apartment.

Mostyn nodded and wondered where the creature could have gone. *Was there a vacant apartment in the building?* he asked himself. *Or has the thing taken up residence somewhere else? If so, this might prove to be a new wrinkle in the case.*

He spotted Doctors Heber and Gerstner and pulled them aside. "Do you know if zuvembies move around?"

"You mean to different locations?" Heber asked.

Mostyn nodded.

"Not generally."

Gerstner nodded his head in agreement. "Not that I've run across," he added.

"Then how do you account for our missing zuvembie?" Mostyn asked.

Gerstner shrugged. "I can't."

"My guess," Heber said, "is that the zuvembie may have

relocated to a more favorable spot. Otherwise, they are rather like bats. They find a place and stick with it."

Gerstner paused for a moment, giving Heber's comment some thought, and then said, "Although bats will change their roosts if threatened by predators, and some have seasonal roosts."

Heber nodded. "True, true. If that's the case, then it may very well be possible for our zuvembie to change digs, so to speak."

Mostyn took a deep breath and exhaled. "Thanks. Not what I wanted to hear, but thanks."

"Boss, I think I may have found something. It was in a purse I found in the bedroom. Sandra Farber apparently had an appointment with a counselor at Asher and Associates in Hoboken." NicAskill handed Mostyn a plastic bag containing the card.

He smiled. "I think you just earned your pay for this week, NicAskill. Good job."

"Thanks, Boss."

After another twenty minutes, or so went by, Jones came up to Mostyn. "We've been through this place six ways to Sunday. Other than what Nicky found, there's nothing here."

"All right, Jones, round everyone up. We're done here for now."

When everyone had filed out, Mostyn told Jones he'd be down in a minute. He walked to the bedroom and looked at the bloodstained bed where most likely Sandra Farber had buried a hatchet in her husband's head.

What had happened that allowed a couple who had once loved each other to come to hate each other instead? Hate each other to the point where one had resorted to becoming a zuvembie in order to kill the other? And why become a zuvembie in the first place? Why hadn't she just killed him?

Mostyn looked at the business card.

Asher and Associates
Family, Marriage, and Children Counseling
2735 S. 8th St, Ste. 304
Hoboken, NJ 07030

In one bottom corner was an email address and in the other a website address.

Mostyn, deep in thought, put the evidence bag in his pocket. He left the apartment, nodded to the police officer, and took the stairs to the main floor. Just before opening the door to enter the small lobby, he asked himself, *What if these women didn't know they were going to become zuvembies?*

6

ZUVEMBIE APOCALYPSE

ON THE DRIVE back to the hotel, Mostyn put in a call to OUP headquarters and asked if there were any business cards for Asher and Associates in the evidence the FBI had collected. He was told someone would get back to him as soon as possible.

Mostyn dialed a second number and, after giving the password, heard, "What may I do for you, Pierce, my boy?"

"Doctor Bardon, we've just discovered the zuvembies may be on the move, or at the very least, some of them may be relocating. Each of the houses where the murders took place needs to be searched to see if the zuvembie is still there or has moved."

"I assume the creature was not at the apartment you were investigating?"

"No, sir, it wasn't."

"Yes, this could pose a problem. Very good. I'll dispatch teams to the other murder sites."

The call at an end, Mostyn pocketed his phone.

"You know, Boss," Jones said, while negotiating the SUV

around a slow-moving semi, "if these zuvembies can move around, what's stopping them from all going back to Van Dyne headquarters?"

"Assuming van Dyne and his company are behind this, nothing at all."

"So instead of the zombie apocalypse, we could be facing the zuvembie apocalypse."

Mostyn chuckled. "I suppose you're right."

Doctor Heber asked, "What or who is this van Dyne?"

"Van Dyne Corporation, owned by Valdis Damien van Dyne, is an international corporation headquartered in New Jersey," Mostyn explained. "They are mainly involved in the biomedical field. At least publicly. Some time ago we ran into them making monsters."

"Monsters?" Heber asked to make sure he had heard Mostyn correctly.

"Monsters," Mostyn affirmed. "We think they were proto-types for a new form of terrorist weapon to destabilize legiti-mate governments and allow Van Dyne Corp operatives to take over."

"They were trying to take over the world?" Heber asked.

"That's it in a nutshell," Baker answered.

Heber ran his fingers through his hair. "So you're thinking these zuvembies are being created by Van Dyne Corporation with the ultimate goal of taking over the world."

"That's what I'm beginning to think," Mostyn said.

"But we have no proof this Van Dyne Corporation is involved," Heber said.

"No, we don't," Mostyn admitted, "but if they are, we'll find out."

"But even if Van Dyne Corporation is behind the creation of these creatures, how can they produce enough to create an apocalypse scenario?" Heber asked, and added, "It doesn't seem likely."

Jones answered, "Good question, Doc. As I see it, maybe this is simply stage one. Create a few of these things and see what happens. Then, if they like what they see, they go to phase two. Maybe contaminate a small town's water supply and see what happens. Some guy wrote a book that had that scenario. Spooky."

"You're referring to a novel, right?" Doctor Able said, a tinge of disdain coloring his tone.

Baker looked over at Able. "So what if Jones gave a fiction example. Makes perfect sense to me. Start with individuals, then take it to the next level: a small town. If successful, roll it out to the big urban centers."

"That's it, Willie Lee," Jones said. "Can you imagine New York with four million of these monsters creating havoc?"

"It's conceivable," Mostyn said. "The population of New York could be wiped out in one night. And then these things fan out and obliterate Newark and Philly. Boston." He shook his head.

Jones nodded. "Half monsters and the other half dead."

Able shrugged. "I'm a parapsychologist. Monsters aren't my normal line of work, but I see your point and it's sounding a bit like the night of the living dead."

"I'm skeptical," Heber said. "Zuvembies are rare. I don't see how this van Dyne person or even the devil could create four million of them."

Jones laughed. "Well, I hope I'm not the one who gets to tell you, 'I told you so.' Because at that point we might be running for our lives." He swung the SUV into the underground garage at the hotel and parked.

As Mostyn got out, NicAskill pulled in next to Jones with

the other team members. When everyone had exited the vehicles, Mostyn told them to be in Conference Room B in fifteen minutes.

Dotty and Helene walked in with Mostyn.

"What did you find out, Dot?" Mostyn asked.

"Not much, other than the usual. Hit with a hatchet while he was sleeping. One blow smashed through the skull and into the brain. I'd say he died immediately. Nothing remarkable or unusual. I understand you didn't find the creature."

Mostyn shook his head. "No, and that's what's troubling me. If these things are going to start wandering around, we could be in for big problems."

"How can we stop them, Mostyn Pierce?" Helene asked.

"I don't know. But first things first. We need to decide if these are isolated cases, or if someone is behind them."

"It's van Dyne," Dotty said, "but what's his game this time?"

"Assuming it's van Dyne," Mostyn said, "I think Jones may have hit on it."

Dotty laughed. "Jones? *Our* Jones?"

Mostyn smiled. "Yes, our Jones. The one and only Greek god look-alike. DC Jones."

"You make fun of DC," Helene said, "but he is actually an intelligent man. However, he does not spend a lot of time thinking. He is a man of action."

"If you say so, Helene," Dotty replied.

"I do, my sister."

Dotty made a face when Helene said, "my sister", which Helene either did not see or chose to ignore. Mostyn was glad. Maybe the two of them were finally settling in to the relationship Bardon had arranged for the three of them. Although Mostyn wasn't sure he was completely at ease with it.

If he had his way, he'd be with Dotty. But Helene was a prize asset and Bardon wanted her happy, and she was happiest when she was with her "husband". Mostyn sighed.

Before either of the women could ask what was wrong, Doctor Roderick Gerstner, the mythologist, caught up with them.

"You know, Mostyn, this case, does it mean we have to, you know, go after van Dyne again?"

Mostyn shrugged. "We have no proof, yet, that van Dyne's involved."

"But if he is, I'd like to be excused from any direct action."

"Cold feet?" Dotty teased.

"Wife and children, Doctor Kemper," Gerstner replied.

Mostyn's phone chimed. He took it out of his pocket and looked at the text. A smile appeared on his face.

"Good news?" Dotty asked.

Mostyn nodded. "Very good news."

7

ASSIGNMENTS

MOSTYN LOOKED over the ten people sitting at the table. All of them had been with the OUP for several years, save Helene. She had the least amount of time with the organization, but had proven herself to be a very valuable asset.

Gerstner, on the other hand, was more and more trying to avoid field work. Mostyn didn't blame him. The guy was looking at fifty and had a wife and kids. He'd have to give the mythologist softer assignments that had little potential for going south.

Doctor Able, with his Sigmund Freud affectation, was another one Mostyn wouldn't want to rely on in a firefight. He'd probably pair him up with Gerstner.

That left Doctors Heber, the cryptozoologist, and von Dampst, the clairsentient and arcane studies expert. Mostyn figured he might need them, which meant he had no choice but to keep them available. Hopefully, those two wouldn't be in the thick of things if a firefight broke out.

All persons connected with the OUP had weapons and

self-defense training. However, as with anything, some were better at it than others.

Mostyn cleared his throat, and in a moderately loud voice said, "Eyes front." Then added, "And that includes you, Ramsey. Put the tablet away."

When Ramsey had his tablet stowed in the ever present backpack, Mostyn continued. "We know we are dealing with a zuvembie in each of the ten murder cases we're working on. We captured one of the creatures, which leaves nine more out there."

"We're assuming each murder was done by one zuvembie?" Able asked.

"Yes," Mostyn said. "Given the geographical separation of the cases, and the limited mobility of the creature, that seems to be a likely scenario."

"Why limited mobility?" Ramsey asked.

"According to Doctor Heber," Mostyn said, "the zuvembie tends to stay put in the place where it was created. Isn't that right, Doctor Heber?"

"Yes, it is. Although we now have evidence that they will move on to a new location if they feel threatened or to pursue other quarry. We must remember the zuvembie's sole delight is in the slaughter of human beings. It is a hate motivated killing machine. There is nothing redeemable about this monster."

"All right, there you have it," Mostyn said. "I just got a text from the agents going through the evidence collected by the FBI. They found two more business cards for Asher and Associates. I think this is the key we've been looking for.

"Doctors Gerstner and Able, you will fly out to Omaha and talk to the Asher and Associates people there. Doctors Heber and von Dampst, you will head out to Seattle and investigate the office there. NicAskill and Baker, you will investigate the Hoboken office. And Willie Lee, I want you to get as many pictures as you can of the place."

"Will do, Mostyn," Baker replied.

"You six can leave now. Jefferies will make sure whatever you need will be at the OUP office in your destination city. Gerstner and Able, your flight leaves in about six hours. The same for you two." Mostyn pointed to Heber and von Dampst. "Don't be late. You'll report back to headquarters, ASAP."

The six left and Mostyn looked at Jones, Ramsey, Helene, and Dotty.

"What do you want us to do, Mostyn?" Dotty asked.

"I want you and Helene to visit our zuvembie prisoner, the former Kelsey Thomas. You'll catch a helicopter at the airport."

"Uh, did you forget?" Dotty said. "I work with dead people."

"No, I didn't forget," Mostyn replied. "And you may get your chance yet. But for now I want you to use your knowledge of anthropology and tell me what you see when you observe the zuvembie. And you, Helene, I want you to try to talk to it."

"Yes, Mostyn Pierce."

Dotty looked at Helene. "Do you always have to be so damned agreeable?"

Helene smiled. "It is a new experience."

Mostyn laughed, and Dotty rolled her eyes. Jones smiled, and Ramsey simply had a bored look on his face.

"You're right, Helene, it will definitely be a new experience," Mostyn said. "Now off with you two."

Dotty shook her head and followed Helene out the door.

"And then there were three," Jones said.

"Right, Agatha," Mostyn replied. "Ramsey, I want you and your drones to run surveillance on Van Dyne Corp's head-quarters."

"What am I looking for?"

"Anything and everything. But, specifically, anything you might find that will shed a little light on our case."

"Can do."

"Good. Get going."

Ramsey grabbed his backpack and left.

"You and I, Jones, are going to investigate Asher and Associates."

"You mean we have to stay inside?"

"Yep."

Jones looked downcast.

"Cheer up, Jones. We'll get room service. How does that sound?"

"And Herndon will be okay with that?"

"Doesn't have much choice. We're working. Now let's see if Asher and Associates has an owner named Valdis Damien van Dyne."

8

DECEPTION AND DISAPPOINTMENT

WHILE MOSTYN and Jones were getting comfortable for a long night of research, NicAskill and Baker drove to Hoboken and parked down the street from the building where the offices of Asher and Associates were located.

They got out of the SUV and walked to the building, found the floor they needed, and got in the elevator. When the doors slid open, the two made their way to the office and entered.

Baker walked around the waiting room taking pictures with a tiny camera disguised as a lapel pin on his sport coat, while NicAskill talked with the receptionist.

"Hello. I'd like to see the owner, or office manager," NicAskill began.

"We're just a branch office of Asher and Associates," the smiling, pretty little redhead said, "and there's no office manager. Just myself and the therapist, Kashvi Pushpagiri. I haven't seen you here before. May I ask what you are looking for?"

NicAskill showed the young woman her ID, which said she was with the Commerce Department.

The redhead said, "Oh. The Commerce Department? Are you investigating something?"

Baker stood next to NicAskill and stuck a microphone and transmitter on the underside of the counter separating them from the receptionist.

"Is Ms. Pushpagiri in?" NicAskill asked.

"No, she's not. Would you like to make an appointment?"

"No. We don't have time for that," NicAskill replied. She took an aerosol can, about the size of three pencils rubber banded together, out of her pocket and sprayed a fine mist in the receptionist's face.

"What the..." The receptionist's eyes rolled back in her head and her body slumped against the chair back and then fell over onto the floor.

Baker stepped over to the door, shot the dead bolt, and turned the lock on the knob. Over his shoulder, he said, "I'll take care of her. You do your thing."

NicAskill opened the door to the back area and walked down the corridor looking for the therapist's office. She found it, the first door on the left, but continued on down to the end, opening the other three doors. Two rooms were empty, and the remaining one looked to be a supply room.

She walked back to the room that had Pushpagiri's name on the door, and entered. There was nothing out of the ordinary to see. The room had a desk, bookshelves, credenza, couch, and chairs.

NicAskill took a look at the wall-mounted bookshelves. Books, multiple copies of some titles, filled the three shelves. There was a credenza below the bookshelves with two cupboards. She opened the sliding doors, first one side, then the other. Boxes of tea. Hotplate. Cups and saucers. A couple of tea pots.

She slid the doors back in place and went to the desk, sat, and opened drawers. There were several tablets of paper, a collection of gel pens, a pile of paper clips, a stapler, various forms, a couple pairs of shoes, and a makeup bag. Nothing unusual. She turned on the computer, which was one of those all-in-one models. On the screen was a message asking for the passcode.

"Damn. I don't have time for this." NicAskill thought for a moment, then shut the machine down, unplugged it, picked it up, and left the office.

Baker had tied up the young woman, and was trying to get into her computer, but with no luck.

"Shut the thing down and take it," NicAskill said. "We need to get back to headquarters so the IT geeks can get into these things."

"Righto," Baker replied, and shut down the computer. He yanked the plug and picked up the machine. "What about fingerprints?"

"Forget wiping. They won't be able to track us."

Baker nodded, and the two left the office. Once in the SUV, Baker texted Mostyn to let him know what happened and that he and NicAskill were on their way to DC.

"Now let's hope we can get something out of those computers before the owner discovers they've gone missing," NicAskill said.

"And remotely wipes the data," Baker added.

———

Mostyn stretched and looked at the clock. NicAskill and Baker should be halfway to DC. He and Jones, connected to the OUP computers, had been searching the official government records, the digital paper trail, to see if they could track down an owner for Asher and Associates. And after three hours, they hadn't had much luck.

The supposed founder, according to the website, Doctor David P. Asher, didn't exist. They'd looked at two hundred and sixty-seven David P. Ashers, and none of them fit the bill.

Jones, in particular, was disgusted. "That means this whole thing's a fake."

"The company?"

"Yeah."

"Not necessarily. The company could be a legitimate legal entity. Perhaps Asher's a bit like Colonel Sanders."

"He sells chicken?"

"No, Jones. He's mostly legend."

"Sure. Gotcha."

"See if you can find any legal status for the company," Mostyn told him.

"Okay. What are you going to do?"

"Look at this a different way."

"Okay, Mr. Cryptic."

"Have to maintain my mystique."

Mostyn started with the Hoboken location and looked up who owned the building. He scored right away. Brooklyn Land Management.

Now, who owns you? Mostyn thought.

After no more than fifteen minutes, the trail led him to Simon's Properties Group. Which in turn was owned by Ireland Dream, a corporation registered in the Ukraine, which was owned by The DVD Company. DVD was incorporated in Vanuatu by the Port-Vila branch of Reece, Rice, Fisher, and Asher Attorneys-at-Law. The headquarters was located in New York City.

Mostyn sat back. "Now we know where the name Asher came from." He explained what he'd found to Jones.

"How does that help?" Jones asked. "If the law office that set all this up is in New York?"

"Not sure. However, we might know more if we knew who their clientele is."

"You think Van Dyne Corp used them?"

"It's a thought, Jones."

Mostyn's phone chimed. He took it out of his pocket and looked at the text message.

"You don't have your happy face on."

"That's because I'm not too happy at the moment."

"So what happened now?" Jones asked.

"The search teams had a bit of a problem. We lost two agents. We did capture the former Janelle Peterman and killed three of the creatures."

"Are you telling me they didn't find the others?"

"That's what I'm telling you. There's still five of those things out there somewhere. Just waiting to kill people."

9

SINGING HER WORDLESS SONG

MOSTYN AND JONES had finally called it a night. They turned in to catch a few hours of sleep before the drive back to DC.

While the two OUP agents were pursuing the digital paper trail, a tanker truck had driven from southern New Jersey, through Delaware, and across Pennsylvania to the sleepy borough of Oldenburg. The little town, located near the New York border and Allegheny National Forest, was just an hour from Erie. A quiet hamlet of less than two thousand people, some of whom worked in Erie, and some locally. About half of the adults were retired.

The driver and his companion didn't care about statistics. Nor did they care about the scenery, even if they could have seen it. The headlights of the tanker, even on high beam, didn't illuminate much beyond the highway. They had but one thought on their minds: deliver the cargo in Oldenburg, return to New Jersey, and pick up the rest of their money. Fifty thousand in small bills were already in their pockets, and another two hundred Gs were waiting for them when the job was completed.

Sweet deal, the driver mused. *A quarter mil just to dump a load of chemicals in the water.* Once he got back and got his money, he was off to a remote island beach where he'd spend the next few months, doing nothing more than drinking, smoking cigars, and screwing chicks with big knockers. Of course, he'd have to get rid of his partner. That went without saying.

Upon entering Oldenburg, the driver negotiated the big rig onto a street that fronted the creek, drove three blocks, and stopped in front of the borough's water plant.

"Man, this place is deader than dead," the partner said.

"Yeah, I'm surprised I still see the sidewalks."

"What?"

"Never mind. You're too young." *And too dumb,* the driver said to himself.

While his partner got the hose ready, the driver walked over to the padlocked gate. He looked at the lock, returned to the tanker, grabbed the bolt cutters out of the toolbox, and in a moment the gate was open. He walked on down to the creek, and, with the help of a flashlight to augment the plant's lighting, examined the pipes that took in water from the creek, and followed the pipeline to the filtration unit, and then to the cistern where the water was held.

The driver studied the manhole cover on the cistern, walked back to the tanker, exchanged the bolt cutter for a crowbar, walked back to the cistern, and pried open the heavy cover. He leaned over the edge and played the flashlight beam into the hole. A few feet below the opening lay the surface of the water.

This will be easy, he thought, *as long as no cops or busybodies show up.* No houses lined this portion of the street, and seeing that the time was two in the morning, he didn't think busy-bodies would be likely.

He walked back to the tanker and helped his partner drag the hose to the cistern opening. With the hose in place, he returned to the tanker and turned a valve. The contents of the huge truck began pouring into the cistern.

Leaning against the door to the cab, he lit the stub of a cigar. He hoped this outfit had more jobs for him. There was nothing better than easy money.

When the cigar had been smoked out, he dropped it to the ground and stepped on it. At the same time, a pair of head-lights began making their way down the street. The driver cursed and walked out to meet the patrol car.

The officer stepped out of his vehicle. "What are you doing here?"

"Evening, Officer. We're chlorinating the water."

"We've never had a tanker come in here to do that before. I need to see some ID."

"Sure, Officer. Let me grab the paperwork." He stepped over to the cab and opened the door. The police officer followed, but remained a good ten feet behind the man.

The driver rummaged in the cab for a few moments and then turned around, a silenced pistol in his hand. He pulled the trigger twice. Two forty-five caliber bullets hit the officer who fell backwards as though pushed by a big invisible hand.

The driver walked over to the squad. It was empty. He smiled. "Gotta love the sticks," he muttered. "Where else would you find a solo in a squad?"

He drove the big sedan to the edge of the creek. With the help of his partner, they dragged the body of the cop to the car, and put it in the driver's seat. With the transmission in neutral, the two men pushed the car over the concrete embankment and into the creek.

The driver started the pump on the tanker to speed up the flow, and in an hour and a half the tanker was empty.

"Get the hose wheeled in," the driver said. "We need to get out of here. I'm surprised they haven't sent out another squad to investigate."

His partner worked on rewinding the hose, while the driver replaced the manhole cover.

He walked back to the truck. His partner was finishing up stowing the hose.

"Do you know what this is all about?" the partner asked.

"Nope. Just doing what I'm getting paid for."

"What *we're* getting paid for."

"Nope." And the driver took out the silenced forty-five and fired two rounds into the other man.

The force of the bullets slammed him up against the truck, and then he fell to the ground.

"Like I said. What *I'm* getting paid for."

———

Mostyn and Jones hit the road early, before the sun was up, because Mostyn wanted to get back to DC by mid-morning, and the drive was over four hours long.

"What I don't get, Boss," Jones said, "is what's the point? I mean, you'd need millions of these zuvembies to create an apocalypse. How's that going to happen?"

"You give the Black Brew to enough women."

"The only way to do that is through the water supply. But if you do that, how do you keep it concentrated enough to be effective?"

"I don't know, Jones. My guess is that we've caught whoever is doing this early in their game plan."

"Good for us, I suppose."

"Hopefully." Mostyn's phone chimed, and he checked the message. "Good. We got into Reece, Rice, Fisher, and Asher's computer system. They're feeding me the live link now."

Mostyn opened his laptop and activated the mobile internet connection. In moments, the law firm's content menu on their server filled his screen. He clicked on the clientele files and began looking for any names that might provide a clue who was the ultimate owner of the building.

"They have quite a few clients," he said. "This is going to take a while."

After scrolling through the firm's past clients, Mostyn scanned the list of clients the firm currently had on retainer, and followed that up with a look at the firm's active cases. Nothing jumped out at him.

He sent a text back to headquarters asking that the research people dig into every single one of the firm's clients, with emphasis on the corporate ones.

Mostyn disconnected the link to the OUP computer and closed the laptop.

Whoever owned that building had done his or her best to hide their ownership. Who would go to that much effort? While it wasn't concrete proof, Mostyn felt it qualified as circumstantial evidence that the only one with the resources and need to go through all that trouble was Van Dyne Corporation. Which meant that once again they were going to go head-to-head with Valdis Damien van Dyne.

———

The empty tanker truck pulled into the abandoned industrial park south of Newark. The address sent to the driver via text message while he was en route back to New Jersey. His instructions were to leave the rig in the parking lot for Atlantic Tool and Die Company. His money would be in the black sedan parked right in front of the building. The car keys would be in the ignition.

The driver pulled up to the abandoned business and stopped the truck. He saw the car off to the right. He got out of the cab and walked towards the sedan. The morning air was cool on his skin, but the sun felt warm.

In the doorway of Atlantic Tool and Die stood a young woman. The driver gave her a wave. She, however, gave no response and just looked at him.

Is that an axe in her hand? he asked himself. He quickened his pace. *Best get to the car, just in case she's a psycho.*

He kept his eye on her while she at the same time watched him. *Just my luck to have a nut job shacking up in the abandoned building where they parked the car with my money in it.*

Just as they said, the keys were in the ignition and on the passenger seat sat a large black bag. He circled around to the driver's side and as he reached for the door handle the woman opened her mouth and a weird, yet sweet, wordless song came forth.

The truck driver's mind went blank, and he froze, hand reaching for the door handle. He felt his brain sink into a deep darkness, a darkness blacker than any physical darkness he'd ever experienced.

How long the darkness, the inky blackness, obscured and obliterated his senses, the trucker didn't know. He was in a place with no time, no dimensions, no sensations.

A sense of motion, of movement, his movement, woke him

from his stupor and he heard that wordless vocalize, that sweet and at the same time weird melody. He was moving towards it, walking towards the source of that wordless song. The song that now turned to mocking him. A weirdly mocking song with no words, only a voice — her voice. The voice of that woman, the one holding the axe. He was walking towards her. And in her hands, her black-taloned, claw-like hands, was that axe. And gradually, she raised it high above her head.

No, he screamed. *No!* But the words only sounded in his mind.

He had to get in the car. Get in and drive far, far away. But he was walking away from the car. Away from safety. And what was he walking towards? He saw that what he thought was a young woman was in fact not a young woman at all, but a mockery, a horrible mockery of a woman. It wasn't even human, it was a thing.

Around her a light began to glow as from flickering flames. God, he had to turn around and run away, but he couldn't. His legs wouldn't obey the command his brain was giving them. He was only a few feet away now from the thing. The thing from hell.

The song stopped, and the ghastly yellowed face broke into a smile, a hellishly hideous smile. And he saw the axe coming towards him in a blur. A terrifying blur.

10

CONNECTIONS

MOSTYN SAT in his office contemplating his next steps. There were people examining the law firm's clients. Gerstner, Able, Heber, and von Dampst were on their way back to DC. NicAskill and Baker had turned over the computers to the techies, who were now doing their thing with the machines.

Dotty and Helene were interrogating the prisoner. At least as much as anyone could interrogate something that was no longer human. And once the bodies of the three zuvembies were in the lab, Dotty would have something to cut up, and that would make her a very happy camper.

That left Ramsey and his drones. Mostyn hadn't heard from the geeky agent. Which wasn't totally out of character for Ramsey, as he tended to do his own thing. However, a word would've been nice.

Mostyn reached for his phone and sent a text to the agent asking him to report. He checked his watch. There was enough time to catch lunch before the afternoon meeting he'd called. He shut down his computer, grabbed his fedora, and left the office.

The elevator deposited him in the underground parking garage where he retrieved his car: a vintage 1969 AMC AMX in Matador Red, with a double white stripe running the length of the top of the car. In its day, it was the poor man's Corvette.

He drove over to Bernie's Deli, a hole-in-the-wall eatery within walking distance of the Congressional office buildings. Not that many elected officials ate there, but many of their staff did. It was one of the best places in town to pick up gossip.

Mostyn parked his car, walked in, and ordered a corned beef on rye with extra pickles, kraut, and Bavarian-style mustard. He also got an iced tea, with plenty of lemon and sugar.

Taking a look around the eatery, he found a table for two along the wall and sat. From out of his suit coat pocket came his phone and an ear bud. He brought up the directional amplifier app and put the ear bud in his ear.

He took a bite of his sandwich, chewed, and let his eyes take in the little deli and its other occupants.

Well, I'll be damned, he said to himself. *That's Miriam Abramowitz, Congresswoman Diane Steinberg's majordomo.*

He turned the phone on the table until the receiver got a lock on the woman. Her voice came in loud and clear. She was complaining about something. Mostyn looked at her lunch companion. The man looked familiar, but Mostyn couldn't place him. He slipped on a pair of glasses, tapped a tiny button on the left bow, and softly said, "Identify."

In a matter of seconds, a dossier appeared before Mostyn's eyes. "Well, I'll be...," he muttered, took a bite of his sandwich, and listened to their conversation.

"Your boss is still the chair of the Crime, Terrorism, Homeland Security, and Investigations subcommittee, isn't she?" the man asked

"She is," Abramowitz answered.

"Then I don't see what the problem is. Our boss wants to make sure this Bardon is put out of action before he learns too much."

"He's not my boss."

"Oh, my dear Miriam, I'm afraid he very much is your boss. In fact, he's the boss of many here in Washington. It will take only one or two phone calls and Ms. Steinberg will be forced to resign and you will be out of work. No, he's your boss as much as he's mine. You and I are the devil's demons, so to speak. So as I was saying, once again, Bardon is getting too close and must be stopped. Today would not be too soon."

"Look, Mr. Tarantolo, we can't find any Rafe Bardon on the government payroll. And we can't find any Office of Unidentified Phenomena, either. Maybe your boss is paranoid."

"He's not paranoid. He knows Rafe Bardon exists. He's talked with him, and he knows the agency Bardon directs exists. It is time, my dear Miriam, you start sleeping with the right people — instead of the wrong ones — because our boss wants action *now*. Do you understand?"

Mostyn watched Miriam Abramowitz nod her head.

"Good. Now you and Ms. Steinberg had best get to work." The man stood. "And if you aren't spending the night with someone who can tell you all about this Rafe Bardon, I will expect you at my place nine o'clock sharp." He placed a card on the table and left.

Miriam said, "Shit", and got out her phone.

Mostyn adjusted the app so he could hear the phone conversation.

"Yes, Miriam?"

"They want us to track down this Bardon guy again and that damn office he's supposed to run."

"I see."

"I told him we don't think either exists. Tarantolo says *he* thinks they exist, so they exist."

There was silence, and it lasted long enough for Miriam to ask if Steinberg was still there.

"I'm here. Come back to the office. We need to figure out a game plan."

"I'm on my way."

The call ended, Miriam put money on the table, and left.

Mostyn, a large smile on his face, took a bite of his sandwich.

So Vinnie Tarantolo was putting the squeeze on the congresswoman. That was confirmation enough for him. He also remembered where he'd seen the guy. Eight years ago, when Mostyn was with the FBI. Since then, both of them had gotten new bosses. Mostyn had gotten Bardon, and Tarantolo had gone to work for Valdis Damien van Dyne.

11

DISCOVERIES

Everyone, except for Agent Ramsey, was sitting in the conference room. Ramsey's absence weighed on Mostyn's mind. The agent hadn't replied to his text asking him to report. And even for Ramsey, that was unusual. Mostyn already considered the agent to be missing in action.

He took a deep breath, exhaled, and began the meeting. "The purpose of this meeting is to catch everyone up with where we are at in the investigation."

Jones interrupted. "Where's Agent Geek?"

"I don't know," Mostyn replied. "He hasn't responded to my request for him to call in and report."

"Sounds to me he's MIA," NicAskill said.

Mostyn nodded. "Likely."

A red alarm light began flashing and a soft British-sounding female voice said, "Intruder alert. Main entrance." The message kept repeating without interruption.

"Jones, NicAskill, you're with me," Mostyn said. "The rest of you stay here."

The three agents ran to the stairwell, down the stairs to

the main floor, and continued out onto the mezzanine where they saw Agent Carter Ramsey suspended fifteen feet above the floor in a greenish haze.

It was only the second time Mostyn had seen the Level 10 Spiritus Sanctus in action. A smile touched his lips. The names Bardon assigned to the inter-dimensional beings that at times worked for the OUP were often whimsical.

But nothing about this spirit was holy. The other time Mostyn had seen it in action, it had slowly eviscerated three OUP staff because its blood payment had been late.

Bardon appeared by Mostyn's side. "Well, our lost little lamb has returned."

Mostyn cast a sideways glance at his boss and asked himself, *How did he know Ramsey was missing in action?* He hadn't said anything to Bardon and had just informed his team. But that was Bardon for you. He seemed to know everything.

"Yes, sir, it looks as though he has."

"Unfortunately, he's been compromised. We'll undoubtedly find a bio-based tracker somewhere in his body."

"Probably," Mostyn agreed.

"He was conducting surveillance at Van Dyne Corporation's headquarters. Correct?"

"Yes, sir."

"That means they've tracked him here."

Mostyn told Bardon about Miriam Abramowitz's lunch with Tarantolo.

Bardon sighed. "This building's location will get passed on to the congresswoman and we will have unwanted visitors. I'm sure of it."

"You're undoubtedly right, sir."

Bardon sighed again. "I'd best see about maintaining our invisibility. I'll find you a replacement for Mr. Ramsey."

"Thank you, sir."

Bardon turned and walked away. Mostyn looked back at Ramsey suspended in the air. A question bubbled up in Mostyn's mind about the blood for the Spiritus Sanctus. Where did it come from? After a moment's thought, he decided he didn't want to know.

———

After sending Jones and NicAskill back up to the meeting room, Mostyn watched with interest as security coaxed the Level 10 security daemonus into letting Ramsey go. The agent was then whisked off to a secure medical facility for examination.

This was the end of any field work for Carter Ramsey. If he was medically capable, he'd spend the rest of his days flying a desk. He might be a remote drone operator, and for Ramsey's sake Mostyn hoped that would be his assignment.

If he wasn't capable of desk work, he'd be retired, given a new persona, and spend the rest of his days under constant observation in a location far off the beaten path to anywhere. If there was a God in heaven, Mostyn hoped Ramsey could at least handle a desk, if not a joystick.

After security had taken Agent Geek away, Mostyn went back to his meeting. He briefed his people on Ramsey and then listened to their reports. The findings weren't overly encouraging. The Asher and Associates offices in both Omaha and Seattle were closed.

Gerstner and Able went so far as to break into the Omaha office, which Mostyn found surprising given Gerstner's recently voiced reluctance to go toe to toe with the Van Dyne

Corp. For their efforts, they'd found nothing except bare rooms.

Neither Gerstner and Able, nor Heber and von Dampst were able to track down an owner or manager for the buildings in which the Asher and Associates offices had been located. That information didn't surprise Mostyn.

Dotty and Helene had attempted to communicate with the captured zuvembie, but to no avail. The creature didn't respond to Helene's telepathy or Dotty's more direct forms of communication. They'd given up after a couple hours. Dotty, however, looked forward to doing autopsies on the dead zuvembies. Nothing like being on your own turf.

"So where does that leave us, sir?" NicAskill asked. "I mean Ramsey seems to be proof positive that Van Dyne Corporation is behind this new crop of monsters, doesn't it?"

"It's proof enough for me," Jones said.

"I want to wait for the report on who owns the building in Hoboken," Mostyn said. "If ownership can be traced to van Dyne or his corporation, then we're good. Valdis Damien van Dyne is well-connected — and I do mean *well*-connected. We don't want to screw up."

"So are we just going to sit and do nothing?" Jones asked.

"No, Jones, we aren't," Mostyn replied.

There was a knock on the door, and Evelyn, Bardon's secretary, entered. Although Mostyn was convinced Evelyn was more than a mere secretary to Bardon, what that "more" entailed Mostyn couldn't even begin to hazard a guess.

"Sorry for the interruption, Special Agent in Charge Mostyn. Doctor Bardon would have come himself, but he is busy distracting the US Marshalls who are here to serve a Congressional subcommittee subpoena."

"That was fast," Mostyn said.

"Very fast. Caught Doctor Bardon by surprise, and you know that rarely happens."

"True, it doesn't."

"Research and Analysis has finally located the owner of your building."

"Wonderful," Mostyn said, although the look on his face was wary. "Am I going to like this owner?"

"I think so." Evelyn smiled. Mostyn had always thought she had the prettiest smile. "The owner is Hadria Clovinia van Dyne. Mr. van Dyne's sister."

12

IT'S IN THE WATER

THE AUTOGYRO FLEW across the Pennsylvania countryside at an altitude of twenty-five hundred feet. Mostyn looked out the window at the rolling farmland, villages, and large expanses of woods that covered the earth beneath them. With him were Jones, NicAskill, and Helene. Although Helene wasn't visible. She'd had to dematerialize in order to fit in the four-seater aircraft.

The four of them had been en route to Van Dyne corporate headquarters, when Sumer Base, the code name for Mostyn's mission handler, had redirected them. Not far from the Delaware border, the team had swapped the SUV for the autogyro.

Mostyn looked at his tablet. They were on their way to the little borough of Oldenburg. Not even two thousand people called the village home. And if the reports were correct, there were at least three or four dozen fewer people calling the place home as of earlier in the morning. And there would probably be more by the time he and his team got there. The rest of his team were already on their way and would probably arrive in the small town before he did.

According to the report Mostyn had received, the County Sheriff and the State Highway Patrol had cordoned off the town to prevent anyone going in or coming out after the first half-dozen murders had occurred. Shortly after the action by county and state officials, word had gotten to Bardon, and he quickly claimed jurisdiction.

However, Mostyn wasn't sure he and his people were any better equipped to handle the situation than the county and state people.

Lead and steel. That is what would destroy the zuvembies, and that's what Mostyn was sure they were up against. Somehow his worst fear, he felt, was now being played out. Contaminate the water supply, and every woman who drinks becomes a monster.

"Isn't this something of a waste of time, Boss?" NicAskill asked.

"Yeah, why can't the state boys take care of it?" Jones added.

"My guess is Bardon wants to keep a lid on what's going on. Think about it. If word gets to the media, there could be mass panic. Which is exactly what van Dyne wants. He's a megalomaniac."

"But aren't the locals going to talk when they find out the Feds pulled rank?" NicAskill countered. "That's sure to raise suspicions."

Mostyn shrugged. "I don't disagree, but this decision is coming from above my pay grade."

"That's how it always is," Jones said. "Good thing we're still packing the lead semi-wadcutters, because we're probably going to need them."

The autogyro landed on the highway just inside the police cordon. Mostyn stepped out, followed by NicAskill, Jones, and the rematerialized Helene. Mostyn asked her if she was okay.

"I am fine, Mostyn Pierce. Another new experience. Our world is so exciting!"

"I suppose it is," he replied.

A man in a State Highway Patrol uniform walked up to Mostyn. "You people reporters?"

"No," Mostyn replied. "I'm Special Agent in Charge Mostyn. We're with FBI intelligence." Mostyn showed the officer his ID.

"Do you know what's going on?" the Highway Patrolman asked.

"I'm not at liberty to say," Mostyn answered. "Any reporters been here?"

"Not yet. Been expecting them, though."

Mostyn nodded. "Keep them away. This is top secret." He leaned in close to the Patrolman. "If you value your job, the sunshine, and the fresh air, you will *not* allow any reporters near here."

"I understand."

"Good. Did my team arrive?"

"They did. About half an hour or so ago. They've gone on into the town."

"Thanks, officer."

Mostyn turned to Jones, NicAskill, and Helene. "The others are here. Let's go."

He took his phone out of his pocket and told it to call Dotty. When she answered, he asked where they were.

"Town hall," she said. "There are at least a couple hundred

people here all asking the same question: what the hell is going on? The mayor is trying to keep everyone calm, but without much success. Panic is in the air."

"We'll be there in a minute, Dot. Let me lock onto your coordinates."

Mostyn activated the location finder and then ended the call. While he and his teammates made for the town hall, he called in to Sumer Base for instructions on what to tell the good people of Oldenburg and to request an immediate evacuation of the women, and delivery of drinking water.

In five minutes they were at the borough hall. Mostyn estimated there were at least fifty people milling around outside the doors. He, Jones, and NicAskill made their way through the crowd. Helene stayed back and, when no one was looking, dematerialized.

Mostyn chuckled. That was one way to avoid a crowd.

When they reached the top of the steps, he showed his ID to the police officer, and was told to go in. Once inside, he found the building packed with people. The three OUP agents pushed their way through the crowd until they reached the meeting room.

A man was at the microphone and was in the middle of giving the mayor, police chief, and borough representatives a vicious tongue lashing. Mostyn stepped up to him and said, "Excuse me."

The guy looked at Mostyn and told him to wait his turn. Mostyn held up his ID and said in a very loud voice so everyone in the room could hear him, "FBI!"

The man looked at the ID, scowled, and stepped away from the mic. In times like this, Mostyn thought it was good most people deferred to authority. Although in general he found such a docile attitude to be scary, even if it did make his job easier.

He took the mic. "I'm Special Agent in Charge Pierce Mostyn. I and my team are with the Intelligence Branch of the FBI and we are here to help you."

A woman called out, "Thank God!"

Mostyn continued, "In five minutes your mayor and police chief are going to order a round-the-clock curfew. We believe a dangerous pathogen has entered your water supply. Do not drink your water. I repeat: do not drink your water. The government will be delivering safe water to you all soon. And because this suspected pathogen is highly contagious, we need you to stay indoors to avoid spreading it. You all need to leave this building now and return to your homes."

"How did it get here, this pathogen?" someone in the crowd called out.

"I cannot answer any questions. Go home now. Anyone seen on the streets after the curfew has begun will be shot dead. No questions asked. Now go."

The people began filing out of the room, and that's when the eerily weird, yet sweet vocalise began.

13

STOOLIES

MOSTYN QUICKLY PUT earplugs in his ears and began looking for the source of the weird, yet sweet melody. The other members of his team, earplugs in their ears, were doing the same. There were dozens of people still in the meeting room, many more were outside.

The crowd and the city officials all looked to be in a daze and everyone had stopped moving. All was quiet save for the vocalise.

At last Mostyn spotted the source. A large woman, most likely in her late fifties, or early sixties, had taken on grotesquely horrible features. Her hair had changed and appeared to have a straw-like texture. The skin on her face had turned a dirty yellow; and what had once been her hands were now yellowed claws, with black elongated talon-like nails.

There were too many people around her and Mostyn couldn't get a clear shot. Dotty and Jones had spotted her, and both were approaching with knives drawn.

And then the woman-turned-monster vanished and there

was silence. Almost at once the dazed looks were replaced by ones of puzzlement.

Mostyn removed his earplugs and heard a man calling out, "Mary? Mary! Mary, where are you?"

Crap, Mostyn thought, *this isn't going to be easy.*

Doctor von Dampst and Doctor Gerstner made their way over to the man.

Mostyn went to the microphone and repeated the order that everyone needed to go home as soon as possible. Once again the people began moving. Mostyn turned to the city officials and the police chief.

"You need to issue a twenty-four-hour curfew and it must be enforced."

"Wait a minute, Agent...," one of the borough representatives began.

"Mostyn."

"Yes, Agent Mostyn, we can't just lock people up in their homes and shoot them on sight if they venture out."

"Let me tell you something. You've heard of the zombie apocalypse?"

The police chief snorted. "That horror movie crap?"

"Not anymore. That pathogen in the water I mentioned? I wasn't joking. You all know the government tests all manner of secret weapons, right?"

There were numerous nods.

"Well, accidents happen. Most, nearly all, are contained. This is one that got out of the bag. Now issue that curfew and get everyone inside, or else the army is moving in. And do it fast. I have work to do."

"When should the curfew go into effect?" the mayor asked.

"An hour ago. Get moving." Mostyn walked over to his

team members. Von Dampst and Gerstner were just returning from talking with the man who'd lost his wife.

"Where's Helene?" Mostyn asked.

Dotty shrugged. "She disappeared at the same time the zuvembie did."

Mostyn nodded. "Okay. She'll turn up. We need to divide into teams and start going door to door to see where we're at." Mostyn looked at the new guy, Ramsey's replacement. "And you are?"

"Sorry, sir. Parker Jackson." He extended his hand to Mostyn, who took it and shook hands.

"Are you as good as Ramsey?"

"No one is as good as Ramsey, sir. However, I am more personable."

Mostyn laughed. "Jackson, a rock is more personable than Ramsey. Welcome aboard." He looked over his team. "I want us to divide into pairs. Jackson, you will stay here and do your thing with the drones. We'll all be linked. Make sure your headsets are in working order."

Helene walked into the room.

Mostyn looked in her direction. "Did you take care of the target?"

"Yes, Mostyn Pierce."

"The body?"

"Buried."

"Good. Thank you."

"You are welcome, Mostyn Pierce."

"Now let's get to work. Jackson, get your drones going." The agent nodded and left. Mostyn continued. "Doctors Kemper and Gerstner, you will explore the north side. Helene and Doctor Able, you'll take the south. NicAskill and Doctor von Dampst, you have the east end of town. Jones and Doctor

Heber, you're on the west. Questions?" No one had any, and Mostyn told them to move out.

"What are we doing, Mostyn?" Baker asked.

"We'll check out the downtown area and then the water plant."

"You think we're in van Dyne's Phase Two?"

"That's my guess, Willie Lee. Which means he must have some way of monitoring what's going on."

"Electronic?"

"I'm thinking more along the lines of a person or two."

"Yeah. Stoolies are more his style."

"Which also means van Dyne is probably aware we are on the scene."

"Oh, yeah. And that can't be good."

"No. It can't and it isn't."

14

FEEDING TIME

CONGRESSWOMAN DIANE STEINBERG had just gotten off the phone. Her conversation had been with Valdis Damien van Dyne. And he wasn't at all happy with her. Once again, the call focused on Doctor Rafe Bardon. She felt helpless. At least officially, the man simply did not exist. Neither did the supposed Office of Unidentified Phenomena.

"How the hell am I supposed to find them if they don't even exist?" she said to the wall on which hung the photograph of her first day on Capitol Hill.

She thought back to those early days, simple days, when she was going to save the world. Those were golden days. Days filled with the naïveté of youth. Days of innocence.

Now van Dyne owned her and politics had become ugly. The grasping for power, the getting of power, the desperate fight to hold on to power. And all of it to please van Dyne. She no longer mattered. Everything she did was for van Dyne. Everything she had she had because of van Dyne.

What started out pure and innocent, had quickly become

sullied and dirty. Today, these many years later, she was no longer innocent, and she didn't like what she'd become.

She'd leave, but no one left unless van Dyne said so. No one. If he owned you, you did what he said. You had no choice in the matter.

It's not unlike working for a drug lord, she thought. *Once in, there's no way out. At least no way out alive.*

Yesterday turned out to be a complete fiasco. The marshals had been told by "a little round man with an English accent" that they had the wrong address.

"There's no Office of Unidentified Phenomena at this address," he'd told them. And added that the building was leased by the Adam Smith Foundation and the foundation had no Doctor Rafe Bardon on the payroll.

On receiving the information, van Dyne was furious. "That 'little round man' was Bardon, you stupid cow. Now fix this!"

Steinberg came very close to telling the insulting bastard to "fuck off". But the last congressman who'd said that to van Dyne died in a mysterious and fiery car crash. And Steinberg still valued breathing, so she'd said nothing except, "Yes, sir". Although it galled her to do so.

Miriam arranged for two men to break into the building during the night. They'd found a sign on the front door stating the building was closed for renovation. The men entered the building through the garage, after jimmying the pedestrian door, and once inside forced their way through one of the interior doors to gain access to the building. They reported back to Miriam there was nothing in the building. It was completely empty.

When she asked if they'd checked all the floors. They'd told her they'd checked the first three, but with the elevators not working they weren't traipsing up the stairs to check all fifteen floors. Miriam had been pissed, but there wasn't much she could do. Unless she checked those floors herself and that she wasn't going to do. It wasn't worth the risk of getting caught, and Steinberg didn't blame her.

The congresswoman walked over to the window and looked out onto the buildings of the capitol.

How on earth can a building, completely operational during the day, be completely vacant by nightfall? That was puzzling. It didn't add up.

Van Dyne didn't buy the story and told her in no uncertain terms that Bardon had to be stopped. "Or you will be scrubbing toilets for a living, if I even let you go on living!"

She sighed. Who could she lean on? Who was vulnerable? She needed somebody inside the Department of Homeland Security who would leak her the information she needed.

On the other hand, maybe not. There was Rob Epstein. He'd screwed Miriam dozens of times and wanted her to come over to the department as his personal secretary. Perhaps it was time for Miriam to take him up on his offer.

Speaking to the city below, Steinberg, in almost a whisper, said, "If I can't find a snitch, maybe it's time I plant my own."

———

The Saturday afternoon sun was warm, but Vinnie Tarantolo didn't pay any attention to it. He'd walked around the nondescript office building twice. The place was completely and totally unremarkable. He'd tried the front door and found it securely locked. The sign taped on the door informed him the building was closed for renovations, and when he'd peered through the glass, the place appeared to be completely deserted.

So far, that cute piece of ass wasn't lying, he thought. He also knew van Dyne was never wrong. Tarantolo scratched his head. "Somethin' ain't square," he muttered.

Following the path taken by Miriam Abramowitz's people, he walked down the walkway to the door for the underground garage. He couldn't budge the big door for the cars. He walked over to the pedestrian door. The marks indicating the door had been forced open were clearly visible. He pulled on it and the door opened.

Odd, he thought. *Why wouldn't they secure it?*

He entered, closed the door behind him, and walked about thirty steps and stopped. Before him dozens of cars occupied the parking spaces.

"What the hell is going on here? This place is supposed to be empty. That bitch was lying after all."

A short, round man dressed in a dark brown Brooks Brothers suit and homburg stepped out from behind a pillar. Smoke gently curled from the pipe in his mouth.

"No, she wasn't lying, and you are correct, Mr. Tarantolo. This place is supposed to appear empty. However, for you, I've let you pull aside the curtain. Let you take the red pill, as it were."

"Who the hell are you?"

"I am the one your boss wants out of the way."

"You're Bardon?"

Doctor Bardon took a little bow. "Indeed, I am."

Tarantolo took a silenced pistol out of his shoulder holster. "Sorry, I can't stay and chat."

He leveled the weapon at Bardon, who simply said, "Now."

A green mist surrounded Tarantolo before he could get off a shot, and a moment later he found himself lifted off the floor and floating in the air.

"What the hell's going on? I can't see anything."

The swirling haze obscured everything, but Tarantolo's hearing was unaffected and he heard the little round man say, "It's feeding time, Mr. Tarantolo, and I'm very glad you happened along when you did. My pet very much likes fresh fare."

"What the hell?" He pulled the trigger on the pistol. Nothing happened. The gun failed to fire. "Get me down!" Tarantolo screamed.

The words were the last thing he said, for out of the greenish fog a tentacle emerged and forced its way into his mouth. He grabbed it and tried to pull it out, but his hands couldn't get a grip on the slimy surface. He felt the tentacle push its way into his guts, followed by excruciating pain. But he couldn't scream.

The tentacle began withdrawing and, as Tarantolo's world started to go black, he saw his intestines, in the firm grip of the tentacle, being pulled out of his body and disappear into the mist.

15
───────

ON YOUR OWN

OLDENBURG'S BUSINESS DISTRICT, running for a few blocks along Main Street, was deserted. Checking a couple of the stores near at hand, Mostyn found the doors locked. Down both sides of the street, he saw shades pulled behind windows; or, if not the windows, the doors.

He studied the buildings. Quite a few had second and third floors. Some of those buildings, Mostyn reasoned, had to have apartments on those upper stories.

"What's it to be, Mostyn?" Baker asked, while he snapped several photos.

"Let's start on this side, go down to the end of the business district, then come back on the other side. Let's see what there is to see."

The first business was a single story shop. No upper floors. They walked on to the next building, which had three floors. There was no access to the upper floors from the front of the building, which had been built flush to the walls of the buildings on either side of it.

Mostyn stood on the sidewalk, hands on his hips, looking at the door.

"Maybe it would be best if we took the alley," Baker suggested.

Mostyn agreed, and they walked back up the block, turned the corner, walked to the middle of the block, and turned down the alley.

"It is so quiet here," Baker said, "it's doggone spooky."

"Especially knowing what we are up against."

Behind the three-story building iron steps led to the upper floors. Mostyn and Baker climbed the stairs to the second floor. The door was solid wood with no window or peephole. Mostyn knocked. No answer. He knocked a second time. When no answer came again, he tried the door. The knob turned easily in his hand. He and Baker replaced the headsets with earplugs, and Mostyn pushed open the door.

The room, a kitchen and dining area, was dark. Mostyn pulled out his pistol. Baker did likewise. With his left hand, Mostyn felt for the light switch along the wall. When he found it, he turned the light on.

The kitchen had a stove, fridge, sink, cupboards, table, and four chairs. The table was pushed up against the wall, making one chair unusable.

Mostyn motioned for Baker to follow him. Straight ahead was a small living room. A couch, coffee table, TV. Nothing else. On the coffee table was a frozen dinner tray with remnants of what looked like apple cobbler and mashed pota-toes. To the left of the room, a very short corridor led to a bathroom, and two bedrooms. All three doors were open.

Reaching around the corner and finding the switch, Mostyn turned on the bathroom light. Just a sink, toilet, and tub with a shower attachment.

Mostyn moved into the bedroom on his left. Baker started to follow when the door slammed shut in his face. Feeling more than hearing the noise from the door, Mostyn whirled around and sidestepped just in time to miss the full impact of the baseball bat. It grazed his left arm, and the pain caused him to drop his pistol, which discharged upon impact with the wood floor.

The hideous caricature of a woman swung at him again and Mostyn barely missed getting whacked in the ribs. The momentum of the swing caused the monstrosity to twist, so its right side was facing him. Mostyn leaped at it and knocked the creature to the floor. It opened its mouth and he heard the wordless song. One of his earplugs must have come loose.

He got his hands around its throat and choked off the sound. But the thing was strong, and it pried his hands away from its neck. The song returned. Everything swam. Darkness descended on his mind. From far away he heard a crash. Followed by another. The darkness disappeared.

Mostyn found himself looking at the blood pooling around the zuvembie's head and felt Baker trying to get him to his feet.

"Come on, Pierce. You okay?"

Mostyn took the earplugs out. "Yeah, Willie Lee. I'm okay." He stood.

"I could see that thing was singing," Baker said, "and you looked like you were totally zoned out."

"It was as though a curtain was being drawn over my conscious mind, and the thing had the strength of a body-builder. Pulled my hands away from its throat as if I were a five-year-old."

"You sure you're okay?"

"My left arm hurts. Took a glancing blow from the baseball

bat. But it's okay. Not broken. I'll probably have a big old bruise, though. Come on, let's check the other bedroom."

He retrieved his pistol, and the two checked the second bedroom, which was empty. They turned out the lights and left, Mostyn noting the address so the zuvembie's body could be retrieved.

Out on the landing, Mostyn pointed up. "Let's check out the third floor. I want to know if there are any surprises waiting for us."

They put their headsets back on. Jackson's voice informed them a drone had picked up a situation on the north side of town.

Mostyn keyed the open channel. "Dotty, Gerstner. Baker and I are on our way. We'll meet you at the scene of the disturbance."

The two agents ran down the iron stairs. Mostyn asked Jackson to send a map of the fastest route to his phone. When the chime came, Mostyn took a look at the map, another at his surroundings, and told Baker to follow him.

They ran out of the alley, up the street, cut across yards, and were at the source of the disturbance just behind Kemper and Gerstner.

"That was fast, Mostyn," Dotty said. "Need an action fix?"

"Already seen plenty," he replied. "That's why we're here. To give you support."

"Not sure I need any," Dotty replied, taking her firearm out of its holster.

"Better safe than sorry. Baker, you and Doctor Gerstner cover the back." Baker gave Mostyn a lazy salute, tapped Gerstner on the shoulder, and headed for the back of the house.

"Is something wrong, Pierce?"

"One of those things almost bashed my brains out."

"Good God."

"Earplugs in. And make sure they're secure." When the earplugs were in, he gave Dotty the hand signal to follow him.

Mostyn spotted a drone hovering by a window. He pulled his pistol from its holster and tried the door. It was locked. He stepped back and gave the door a kick. It held. He gave it a second kick, and then a third. The door splintered. He put his shoulder to it, and the door gave.

The zuvembie was waiting, and the thing's mouth was open. Mostyn, though, thanks to the earplugs, did not hear its eerie vocalise. His pistol was up and both rounds from the double tap hit the creature. It fell back onto the floor, twitched, and lay still.

Mostyn and Kemper walked through the rooms on the ground floor. There was nothing. He unlocked the back door and told Gerstner to be ready. He motioned for Baker to cover the front door. With the exits covered, Mostyn started up the stairs, Dotty following.

When they were halfway up, a woman appeared at the top of the stairs. At least the thing used to be a woman. A long nightgown covered its thin body. The skin was sallow, and the dark brown hair had the texture of straw. The thing's hands had grown long, black nails that resembled talons. In its hands was a shotgun, which it pointed at Mostyn.

He dropped flat to the stairs, firing his pistol at the same time. The shot was off mark, hitting the monster in the side. The thing twisted from the impact and pulled the trigger on the shotgun at the same time, blowing a hole in the staircase wall.

Dotty fired a double tap from her pistol before the zuvembie could bring the shotgun back on target. The creature jerked from the impact of the bullets and staggered back. Dotty fired again. The lead semi-wadcutter smashed its way through the left side of the sternum and tore through the top of the monster's heart. The thing dropped to the floor, tried to get up, collapsed, and lay still.

Mostyn got up, said, "Thank you", even though he knew Dotty couldn't hear him, and continued the climb up the stairs.

He looked at the creature. Its eyes staring and unseeing. The thing looked no older than thirteen or fourteen. Outside one of the bedrooms another creature lay. A shotgun blast to the chest had killed it. Mostyn figured the thing had probably been someone's wife.

Inside the bedroom, a young boy had little left of his head. A shotgun blast at close range is a gruesome thing. A man, Mostyn guessed him to be the husband and father, had most of his head missing.

Mostyn and Kemper checked the other rooms. They were empty. Mostyn removed his ear protection. Dotty did likewise.

"Jesus, Mostyn. What a nightmare."

He nodded. "It's not pretty, that's for sure. Rather than evacuate the females, I think it would be better to evacuate all the males and quarantine whatever females remain."

Dotty nodded her agreement. "Looks as though the husband may have stopped the wife, but succumbed to his daughters and killed his son."

"And we killed the daughters."

Dotty nodded.

They went back downstairs, retrieved Gerstner, and walked around the front to join Baker. Mostyn gave them the short version of what had happened, keying his mic so the entire team heard. He then called into Sumer Base.

"Langston, here. How's it going, Mostyn?"

"Not good. We need immediate evac of all the surviving males, and a quarantine of the females. Then a systematic search of the town to eliminate the zuvembies. I don't have enough people to do any of this. Requesting a Special Forces unit here pronto."

"Not sure we can do. Problems in Washington."

"What kind of problems?"

"Seems somebody knows something. Bardon's doing damage control."

"Somebody knows something about the OUP?"

"Yep."

"That's too bad. However, we have hundreds of lives on the line here, Langston. An entire town could disappear. What if the media got hold of that?"

"I see your point. I'll do what I can. But for now, you're on your own."

16

EVIL NEVER RESTS

MIRIAM ABRAMOWITZ HAD GOTTEN the text from her boss and sent another off to Rob Epstein asking when she could start as his personal secretary. Within minutes he'd responded and the one-word message read, "Monday."

Forty-five minutes later, Miriam and Epstein were having lunch together at the swanky Red Pepper Grill, just inside the DC border from Coral Hills, Maryland.

"So what made you decide to come work for me?" Epstein asked, after taking a sip of wine.

Miriam smiled at him. "Diane is very demanding. I'm tired of taking her crap and doing all her shit jobs. I think working for you will be far less demanding."

Epstein smiled. "Certainly during the workday."

Miriam smiled back and took a sip of her wine. She set her glass on the table. "I don't have a problem with the after-hours work."

"Good. Because I am anticipating there will be lots of after-hours work."

"One of the benefits of the job?"

"You might say that."

"After lunch, may I see my new office?"

"On Saturday?"

"Sure. I want to see where I'll be working."

He shrugged. "Okay. Why not?"

Miriam smiled. *This is going to be so easy.*

————

High above the Pennsylvania countryside, the large military drone of Turkish origin circled the borough of Oldenburg. In large, lazy circles the drone flew around the town monitoring what was happening on the ground.

Some three hundred miles away, at a palatial estate outside of Vineland, New Jersey, in a room deep underground, sat a man at a control board. He watched the various video displays, his hand on the joystick maneuvering the unmanned drone.

Behind the operator stood a tall, slim, blonde-haired man. He was dressed in black slacks, black turtleneck, black loafers, and black socks.

Next to him stood a slim blonde-haired woman, who was tall for her sex. The top of her head came up to the bottom of the man's chin. She was wearing an off-white maxi-dress, with a thin gold belt at the waist. Her lips and nails were blood red. On her feet were gold-colored sandals.

The two looked remarkably alike.

They watched the activity on the screens with great interest. Occasionally making comments to each other, and then the man would say something to the drone operator.

The woman pointed to one of the monitors. "Look Valdis, those people. Who are they?"

Valdis Damien van Dyne studied the monitor. "I don't know, Hadria, but I suspect they are Bardon's people. This is, after all, the type of thing they investigate. And...," he pointed, "these people have that look about them. Federal agents are all of a type and are easily spotted."

"I hope they don't spoil our fun."

"Unfortunately, they are good at doing that."

"Yes, they are. Aren't they?"

Van Dyne nodded, his right hand slowly stroking his Van Dyke beard.

"There, Mustafa," van Dyne pointed to a screen, "send a small drone there. I want to know what's going on."

"Yes, sir." The operator sent a command to the drone, watched a display, and then said, "Mini-drone launched, sir."

"Good," van Dyne replied.

In moments, a display came to life and showed close-up pictures of the house and the surrounding people.

Van Dyne pointed. "Isolate him. Send his picture to Fritz for identification."

"Yes, sir." Mustafa pressed several buttons and a copy of the image was sent off.

A few minutes later, an answer came back on the display.

"The image is a match for one of the intruders at the Vautier mansion in North Carolina."

"I thought so," murmured van Dyne. To Hadria, he said, "The presence of that man confirms this is an operation of Bardon's Office of Unidentified Phenomena."

"That can't be a good thing, can it, Valdis?"

"Actually, Hadria, I'm rather glad,."

"You are?"

"Yes. They will be a good test for the zuvembies. Will my little pets be able to overcome a foe bent on their destruction?

If yes, then we are ready for Phase Three. If not, then we will have to work on modifying the Black Brew."

"You are so clever, Valdis. Is it any wonder I love you?" She lifted her head and kissed her brother on the lips. He responded by putting his arms around her and pulling her to him. He kissed her passionately.

When she pulled away, she touched his cheek, and said, "I'll see you later, my love."

"You have an appointment?"

"With Olga. She's teaching me some form of the martial arts."

"You can watch the videos later, if you wish."

She kissed her brother's cheek. "I'm so looking forward to being your Josephine."

17

FLIES ON ROTTEN MEAT

MOSTYN LOOKED AT HIS WATCH. The sun would set any time now. Three hours had passed since the zuvembies had caught him and his team by surprise.

After he, Dotty, Gerstner, and Baker had dealt with the zuvembie sisters, the four of them had moved to the house next door. They'd found it empty. Mostyn held a team meeting to figure out a plan of action until the cavalry arrived.

While they were discussing options, the zuvembies had surrounded the place. For three hours Mostyn and his people had been barricaded inside the bungalow. For three hours the monsters had been whistling and singing their wordless songs.

Mostyn didn't know how many of the townspeople had fallen under their spell, but it had to be dozens, many dozens, judging by the body count piling up around the house.

The creatures would sing and whistle, summoning all who could hear. Men, women, and children. It didn't matter. They'd kill the humans and command the lifeless bodies to assault the house until those bodies grew cold, or the blood stopped flowing.

How do you kill a dead person? Mostyn wondered.

A couple hours ago, Jones needed to visit the bathroom, and almost got his head bashed in for the effort. A boy around twelve years of age had smashed the bathroom window and climbed through the opening.

NicAskill, passing by on her way to the kitchen to make coffee for everyone, decided to make sure Jones was okay since he'd been in the room for longer than usual. She opened the door, saw a teenage girl climbing through the opening and Jones struggling with a boy. NicAskill pointed her shotgun and pulled the trigger. The dead girl's head blew apart, and she collapsed on the sill. Using the shotgun barrel, NicAskill pushed the body back out.

While NicAskill was dealing with the girl, Jones had finally subdued the boy and in moments he became truly dead.

To bolster their defenses, Mostyn ordered the team to push as much furniture as they could in front of the doors and windows. The living room picture window, though, because of its size, posed a problem. There just weren't enough sizable pieces of furniture to block off all the points of entry. And when several recently killed people smashed their way through the window, Mostyn decided they'd have to activate one of the Class III Xenophage Defense Apps on their phones.

Gerstner volunteered his phone and activated the app. After the xenophage vaporized several animated corpses, the zuvembies stopped their attempt to breach the house through the window.

Mostyn sent a text to Bardon informing him of the latest developments and discoveries. Doctor Heber was especially excited about the new information.

"This is incredible," he said. "These things aren't mind-less. They can learn."

"Yeah," Jones said, "and that makes them all the more dangerous. I don't understand why you're so excited."

While Heber attempted to explain, Jackson tried a mini-drone swarm to distract the zuvembies, but the maneuver failed. He then sent several drones into the open mouth of one of the things. The drones didn't kill it, but they did stop its vocalise.

NicAskill had tried a stun grenade which had no effect on the zuvembies and definitely none on the newly dead.

After informing Bardon, Mostyn texted Sumer Base on the status of their backup. Langston replied that help was on its way, but the ETA was not for another several hours.

With everyone wearing hearing protection, talking was next to impossible. Texting had worked for a while until concern over the phone batteries curtailed their use for anything other than the most dire of emergencies. Such as activating the defense app.

Mostyn looked at his team and then shifted his gaze to the picture window. Through the greenish haze of the xenophage, he could make out the zuvembies standing there singing or whistling their devilish tunes.

Help was coming, but only God knew when. The upside was that Jackson's drones were sending valuable information back to Sumer Base, which would be analyzed for future use. All that, though, wasn't going to help him and his team now.

We need to talk, Mostyn thought. *Work out a plan of action together.*

They needed to find a place where the zuvembies's sweet melodious songs of death couldn't reach them.

Mostyn tapped Jones's arm and motioned for him to follow

him. The two men took the stairs to the basement. Once there, Mostyn wrote a note on his phone and showed it to Jones. It read:

I will take out my earplugs. If I look like I'm going under their spell, get those plugs back in.

Jones gave Mostyn a thumbs up and Mostyn removed his earplugs. He couldn't hear those damnable tunes. He smiled and motioned for Jones to remove his.

Holding his ear protection in his hands, Jones said, "Never thought the sound of nothing would sound so good."

"Yes, indeed. We're going to meet down here and plan a way out of this mess."

"I'm with you there, Boss. I'm tired of waiting for Langston to get off his ass and do something."

"I don't think it's his fault, so don't be too hard on him. But we do need to be active rather than passive."

"I'm with you there."

"Good. Let's get the others."

Ear protection back in place, they moved upstairs and indicated everyone should head for the basement. And for their protection, Mostyn took Doctor Heber's phone and activated the defense app to guard the doorway. He didn't want any surprises. Such as dead people waiting to bash their heads.

Once downstairs, and with ear protection removed, Mostyn addressed his team.

"We need a plan to get out of here. We have no idea when backup will arrive."

"Why can't we just shoot our way out?" Dotty asked.

"Because we can't kill dead people," Mostyn replied, "and these things have learned to send the dead to fight us."

"What about Ms. Stealth?" Jones said. "She can disappear, reappear next to one of these beauty queens, kill it, disappear, and move on to the next one before they even realize what's happening."

Helene was all smiles. "That is true, Mostyn Pierce. And I will have the hearing protection so I will not be able to hear them. This may be our way of escaping."

Mostyn cast a glance at Jones. *Always happy to volunteer my partner*, he thought. And he didn't like it.

He looked at Helene. Eager as always to help. For her, it was another new experience, and she lived for new experiences. But Mostyn was also concerned that all of the killing would fuel the sadistic side of Helene's K'n-yanian upbringing. And that was something he definitely didn't want.

Doctor Bernard Able, stroking his beard, said, "I don't see what the issue is, Mostyn. Ms. Dubreuil is the most logical choice. Her special ability elevates her above the rest of us." He shrugged. "We can't reason with these things. All that remains is for us to kill them."

"Well, I don't like it," Doctor Heber said.

Doctor Able turned to his colleague. "Why not?"

"Because Ms. Dubreuil is essentially a cryptid herself," Heber replied. "Quite honestly, I'm not sure why Doctor Bardon has let her go out into the field. She needs to be in a safe environment and studied by the finest minds."

Jones scratched his head. "You want to keep her in a cage? She's a person."

"A cage?" Heber said. "No, not a cage. But in a manner of speaking she is no different from any other cryptid. And..." Heber shrugged.

Dotty shook her head. "You're wrong there, Heber. She's a person. A human, just not sapiens."

Heber cleared his throat. "That's precisely why—"

Baker cut him off. "This is nonsense. Doctor Able is right, Mostyn. I know you don't like to always depend on Helene. She's a prized asset. But Bardon wouldn't assign her to the team if he didn't think she was critical to the success of the mission." Turning to Heber, he said, "Which means Bardon doesn't agree with you." He turned back to Mostyn. "And right now, getting out of Dodge is pretty critical on my list of priorities for success."

"We've learned these things adapt," NicAskill said. "Other than the shotgun, we have no long guns with us. These things know to stay out far enough so pistol fire is iffy at best. You, yourself, Boss, have said we're all expendable when it comes to the mission."

Mostyn nodded. "Seems like we're all agreed. Doctor Heber?"

There was a significant pause, before Heber nodded.

Mostyn looked at Helene. "Are you sure you're okay with this?"

"Oh, yes, Mostyn Pierce." She was fairly jumping up and down like a little kid about to enter Disneyland.

He'd never known anyone so gleeful in the face of possible death. He sent his thoughts to her. *You sure you're okay with this? It's not a bit too much like your world?*

Her thoughts appeared in his mind. *Oh, no, Mostyn Pierce. This is a mission. We are not torturing these creatures.*

He nodded and turned to the group.

"Okay, Helene will take out enough zuvembies so we can make our escape." He turned to Jones. "Go up and get a head count on how many of these things we're facing. I want to know how many there are on each side of the house."

"On it, Boss." Jones put in his ear protection and left.

"I'll go with him, Boss," NicAskill said, "to deactivate and reactivate the defense app."

Mostyn nodded his okay. To the rest of the team, he said, "Whichever side of the house has the fewest of these things is where we'll focus our efforts."

"What if they're all equal?" Doctor von Dampst asked.

"Then we'll go out the front," Mostyn replied.

"How are we going to deal with the walking dead?" Dotty asked. "We can't kill them. They're already dead."

"Too bad we don't have anything flammable," Baker said.

NicAskill rejoined the meeting, giving Mostyn a hand signal that all went well.

"The only options left open to us," Doctor Heber added, "is to chill them down so they're no longer warm, or coagulate the blood faster so it no longer flows."

"Or make more wound channels so more blood escapes faster," Baker said. "When the blood is gone, there's nothing left to flow."

"Since they're upright," Dotty added, "gravity will pull the blood towards their feet. That's were we need to make the wounds."

"Too bad we don't have swords," Baker said.

"What about an axe?" NicAskill asked. "There's a wood stove. They must have an axe somewhere."

"There's a meat cleaver in the kitchen," Doctor Gerstner volunteered.

"And a long carving knife," von Dampst added.

"There's probably an axe in the backyard or garage," Baker said.

"I'll retrieve it," NicAskill said, and added, "with your permission, sir."

Before Mostyn could respond, they heard a gunshot and moments later Jones yelling, "Let me in! Let me in!"

NicAskill ran to the phone and deactivated the defense app. She opened the door and Jones came through. She closed the door and reactivated the app.

Jones reported. "The phone died protecting the picture window. Dead people are swarming us like flies on rotten meat."

18

ESCAPE ATTEMPT

MOSTYN and his team heard the floorboards creaking overhead from the footsteps of the zuvembie-animated dead.

"What was the gunshot?" Mostyn asked.

"I was counting," Jones answered, "when the phone died and the xenophage disappeared. A half-dozen corpses started moving towards the opening, and a half-dozen of those things were following at a distance."

Heber was excited and interrupted. "That apparently means a zuvembie can only control one corpse at a time. Oh, this is good news!"

"Yeah, that makes sense, Doc," Jones said, "because I got a chance, a clear opening, and I shot one of those monsters." He looked at Mostyn. "That's the gunshot you heard." He turned back to Heber. "I hit it square in the chest and it dropped like a rock and so did one of the corpses."

Heber looked like a kid on Christmas morning. "They have a limit! They aren't invincible!"

"Nothing is invincible," Mostyn countered. "Everything has a weakness. Just depends on whether or not the opponent knows about it and can exploit it. It seems our Jones has found a weakness. The zuvembie has to be close enough to the corpse to control it, and, in our current situation because they were following the corpses, I'm guessing they need knowledge of the terrain so they can guide the corpse."

"That makes perfect sense, Mostyn," Heber said.

"Like trying to fly a drone blind," NicAskill added.

Mostyn nodded. "Precisely, Kymbra. If you can't see where the drone is going, you're probably going to crash it. Okay, people, we're moving out. Helene, I want you to dematerialize and take out as many of those things in the front yard as you can. Go."

"Yes, Mostyn Pierce." Helene disappeared.

"Jones, NicAskill, and I will lead. We'll use the defense app as a shield. The rest of you follow. Use your defense apps as a shield and keep Doctor Gerstner in the middle because he doesn't have a phone. Dotty, you're in charge. You'll count to five and follow us. Everybody ready?"

There were nods and a murmur of yeses.

"Good. Put in your ear protection."

Mostyn retrieved Doctor Heber's phone from where it lay by the basement door and gave it to him. On Mostyn's signal, Jones went up the stairs first, followed by NicAskill, and then himself.

Jones, surrounded by the greenish glow of the xenophage, came out of the basement. A zuvembie was waiting. The thing plunged a knife towards Jones's heart. The knife and half her arm vaporized. Jones pushed forward, enveloping the zuvembie in the protective halo around him, and it disintegrated.

Jones punched the air and charged into the kitchen. NicAskill and Mostyn followed. They watched him charge into two animated corpses, vaporizing both, and then saw him go after a zuvembie. Before the thing could react, it dissolved in the green glow surrounding Jones.

Another zuvembie swung a meat cleaver at the special agent. The cleaver and the thing's forearm vanished. Mostyn turned off his app and fired his pistol. The lead semi-wadcutter caught the creature in the back. It pitched forward and everything from the waist up disappeared. The rest of the thing's body fell to the floor. He watched its legs twitch for a moment and then lie still.

Jones charged into the living room, heading for the front door, and Mostyn and NicAskill were right behind him. A couple corpses and their zuvembie handlers vaporized in Jones's protective haze.

The trio burst out of the house. NicAskill dropped her defensive shield and opened fire on the few zuvembies that were still in the yard. Mostyn noticed Helene had been at work given the number of the things that were lying on the ground.

He also noticed, in what seemed to be a coordinated effort, that perhaps two dozen of the creatures had fallen back and were in retreat down the street. But the battle wasn't over. In their place, in the growing dusk, hundreds of snakes were slithering up the lawn towards the OUP team, and out of the sky a cloud of bats swooped down on them.

Dotty's group joined Mostyn, Jones, and NicAskill.

"Doesn't this ever end?" Dotty said, swatting at a bat heading for her face. The creature barely missed getting vaporized.

Jones watched a snake disintegrate as it tried to bite him. A bat dived at him and met the same fate.

In the distance, the howls of wolves sounded in the deepening dusk.

Doctor Heber shouted, "They're summoning werewolves!"

"In Pennsylvania?" Dotty said.

Heber sniffed at her ignorance. "There are many cryptids in the less populated areas of Pennsylvania."

"Fall back," Mostyn commanded, and headed back towards the house.

As his team was filing back into the place they'd just left, above the cries of the wolves, came the sound of helicopters and Mostyn saw lights in the sky.

About time they got here, he thought.

And high above the battle, sending back data to a certain mansion in New Jersey, was the large Turkish-made military drone.

19

WHISTLER IN THE DARK

VAN DYNE absentmindedly ate his shirred eggs and toast while watching the videos his drones took of the operation in Oldenburg. Both the large drone and the mini-drones recorded the events, and van Dyne was very much interested in what had happened. The videos played out on a large wall screen at the far end of the long dining room table.

Every so often, he'd make a comment into the digital recorder by his plate concerning what he saw on the screen.

Hadria, sitting next to her brother, sipped a mimosa and nibbled at a crepe with raspberry compote.

"Do you know how many of our lovelies survived, Valdis?"

"Out of a population of one thousand nine hundred and fifty-three, of which fifty-two percent were females, two hundred and thirty-one had transitioned before interference halted consumption of the water."

"Those are very good results in such a short time span."

"Yes, they are, my dear. I have no doubt the results would've been even better if Bardon had not interfered. As for how many of 'our lovelies', as you call them, survived, I do not possess a definitive count. By means of the drones, we tracked thirty-seven that made their escape to the forest. My extraction teams retrieved twenty-eight from the village, and are on their way back to save those that escaped to the forest. There are likely more that survived and are in hiding."

"That is very good. All is not lost then."

"You are such an optimist, Hadria."

"A realist, my love. A realist."

"Very well. A realist."

"Do we know what that green glow is?" She took a sip of her mimosa.

"No. That is a mystery. Whatever it is, it is damn powerful. I would love to get my hands on it. It would make life much, much simpler for us." He reached out and took his sister's hand in his and gave it a gentle, loving squeeze.

Hadria smiled at her brother. "Hopefully that woman will get us the information we need."

Van Dyne made a derisive noise. "I will not be holding my breath. The congresswoman and her aide have proven to be incredibly inept. I will probably have to get rid of them."

"If you decide to do so, please use someone other than Mr. Tarantolo. He is far too crude. I can't see why you hired him."

"You don't have to worry about that, my dear. It seems Mr. Tarantolo has disappeared."

"What do you mean?"

"Just that. He's vanished. Thus far I have not been able to find him. His last assignment was to verify what that Abramowitz woman had told him. He did not return, and he's not been in contact."

"I'm sure you'll teach him a lesson when he does turn up."

"That's the thing, my dear, he was to investigate the OUP

building. He reported arriving, and that's the last we heard from him."

"Send someone else to the building."

"I would, if I could. The problem is the building is no longer there."

———

Miriam Abramowitz, after visiting her new office, which included letting her new boss take her right there on top of her desk, had coaxed Epstein into getting personnel to grant her access to the DHS computer system. That had taken considerable doing, seeing as it was the weekend and she wasn't yet an employee, but in the end Epstein had prevailed.

Now, on this Sunday morning, which Epstein had to spend with his wife and children, Miriam was carefully going through the DHS directory seeing what she could see. Unfortunately, while there were plenty of names and descriptions, nothing about Doctor Rafe Bardon, or the Office of Unidentified Phenomena, appeared to her wondering eyes.

"This is just the shits," she said to the computer screen. "I spend all this time fucking that loser, and there's not a goddamn thing here."

She got up and made herself another rum, cognac, and spiced tea hot toddy. With the steaming hot drink in hand, she walked over to the window.

"My clearance probably isn't high enough," she said. "I'll have to search Epstein's computer." She sipped her drink. "I hope the fucker has a high enough clearance, because I'm really, really tired of faking it and getting nothing in return."

———

Baxter Davidson had lived all of his fifty-eight years in the little village of Irvine, Pennsylvania, which was on the edge of the Allegheny National Forest, and only a couple miles from Oldenburg. The news that something strange was going on in the larger town came from his wife, who'd gotten it from Milly Baum, whose niece lived in Oldenburg.

There was a lot of speculation and even more gossip as to what had caused the town to be quarantined. In the end, though, everyone was in the same boat. They just didn't know.

"I'm really glad Em and Lon are away at school," Baxter said to his wife, and she'd agreed.

"Maybe we should stay with my parents in Erie," Eleanor Davidson suggested.

Baxter shook his head and said that whatever it was that was going on over in Oldenburg, if it was truly bad, the state would give an order to evacuate. Until then, he said, they might as well stay put. And in the end Eleanor agreed with him.

Later on, after supper, while Eleanor was doing the dishes, Baxter took out the garbage. The night was dark, and the stars shone brightly in the sky. One light affixed to the detached garage illuminated the walk. On his way back to the house, the garage light dimmed and then went out. In the starlit darkness, he heard a sweet, yet weirdly eerie melody. No words. Only a tune whistled by someone hidden in the darkness. It was the last thing Baxter heard.

20

COUNTER-OFFENSIVE

DEEP UNDERGROUND, beneath the retail shops along M Street in Georgetown, Mostyn and his team sat in a conference room drinking coffee and eating doughnuts.

Doctor Rafe Bardon was there. He had a pot of tea and his own plate of crumpets and a bowl of orange marmalade. He put his pipe in his pocket and addressed the group.

"Thanks to Agent Jackson's drones, we have a reliable estimate of approximately three dozen zuvembies that escaped from Oldenburg."

"Do we know where they are, sir?" NicAskill asked.

"It appears they took refuge in the national forest. We've put up blockades on all roads leading into and out of the forest. A search is underway as we speak for those creatures. We also know that an unknown number were extracted, we assume by van Dyne, while we were performing damage control in the borough."

"Is there anyone left in Oldenburg?" Baker asked.

"The creatures ended up killing a significant number of persons. We haven't conducted an actual census, but the estimate is that there are between eight hundred to nine hundred survivors. Staff are at the site, erasing the memories of the survivors and replacing them with a believable fiction. Life will be better for all concerned there."

Mostyn thought it will also keep a very big lid on the disaster. *We don't want news of a zombie apocalypse getting out to the media, or the conspiracy folk.*

"So why are we here in this facility?" Jones asked, before taking a big bite out of his jelly doughnut.

Bardon sighed. "The former building was compromised. My attempt to perform damage control was not adequate. The building is now gone. Officially the site has been a parking lot for the past twenty years, and most people won't even remember that a building once stood there. The few who do remember will soon forget. After all, there was nothing remarkable about the structure. Thus all memory of the old place will vanish."

"So now what?" Mostyn asked.

Bardon drank tea and ate a bite of crumpet before answering. "I think it goes without saying that Valdis Damien van Dyne has procured the recipe for the Black Brew, the drink that creates a zuvembie. It also goes without saying he has to date succeeded in manufacturing a large quantity of the brew. What is unknown is if he has any Black Brew remaining with which to conduct further attacks."

"If he does, he could attack anywhere," Doctor Carter Heber said.

Bardon nodded. "Very true. Which is why we need to take the battle to him."

"And how do you propose to do that, sir?" Mostyn asked.

"He had a surveillance drone, of Turkish military origin, observing the borough of Oldenburg. He witnessed our operation in action and now knows even more about us. For our part, we know where his drone landed and we know where the machine sent back its video: a very large home in southern New Jersey, owned by Van Dyne Corporation."

"So are we going to attack him?" Jones asked, a gleam in his eye. "Say around two in the morning?"

Bardon's face took on the demeanor of an indulgent father. "Something like that, Special Agent Jones. We've been monitoring the Van Dyne Corporation headquarters since Agent Ramsey was compromised. Also under surveillance is the mansion in southern New Jersey. It is believed that is where van Dyne makes his home. There also appears to be a large subterranean complex below the house."

"But we don't know where the Black Brew is being manufactured," Mostyn said.

"You are correct, Special Agent Mostyn, we do not."

"If I may, sir?" Mostyn asked.

Bardon indicated he should go ahead.

"I'd wager he was making the Black Brew at the labs in the headquarters building, because that is where they conduct most of the initial experiments."

"But he's already made two tests, and both appear to have been successful," Dotty said. "He may have now moved on to one of his manufacturing sites."

"All true, Dotty," Mostyn replied. "And he may be gearing up to move on to the next phase. However, his large-scale test was still relatively close to New Jersey. I'm willing to wager that he's still making the brew at the labs in the headquarters building."

"Then that is where you shall focus your efforts, Mr. Mostyn," Bardon said. "I will arrange for another team to neutralize the command center at the mansion. If you need anything special for this phase of your mission, inform Jeffries."

"Yes, sir."

"I will now leave you to do what you do best. A good day to you." Bardon stood and left.

Mostyn's eyes moved over the people seated at the table. This part of the operation was going to require people who had good nerves and would not flinch at danger. He spoke.

"For this next phase, we are going to have to penetrate the defenses at Van Dyne Corp, and they are considerable. NicAskill and I have been there before. The place is heavily guarded by things that make those horror movie monsters look like kittens by comparison."

"Are all of us going?" Doctor Roderick Gerstner asked.

"No," Mostyn replied. "I'll take five with me. I want to infiltrate the building at three different locations so we can neutralize the ability of the guards to respond and have a better chance of finding where the Black Brew is being manufactured."

Mostyn took a sip of coffee. "Jackson, you'll be our eye in the sky."

"You aren't going to make me fly in that blimp, are you?"

Mostyn smiled. "Bardon's Folly is very reliable and from there you can launch your drones and keep us informed."

Jackson shook his head. "Yes, sir." His voice indicated he was none too happy with his assignment.

"On the ground with me," Mostyn continued, "will be Jones, NicAskill, Dubreuil, Kemper, and Baker. The rest of you will be with Langston at Sumer Base, in case we need to draw on your expertise."

"Can we get something other than those earplugs?" Jones asked. "They were a major pain in the butt."

"I believe Jeffries has something for us," Mostyn replied. "Any questions?" Mostyn scanned his team's faces. No one indicated they had one. "Very well, you're all dismissed."

When it was apparent Mostyn wasn't leaving the room, Dotty asked if he was coming.

"No, go on," he replied. "I have something I need to check."

"Sure, Pierce. See you at home."

"I'll be there in a bit."

Dotty left and Mostyn pulled up Doctor Carter Heber's profile on his laptop. There was something not quite right about the good doctor. Starting with his comments about Helene being a cryptid and needing to be in a lab, to the way he always looked at her. And it wasn't a look of desire.

21

ULTIMATUM

CONGRESSWOMAN DIANE STEINBERG had been summoned. She'd stepped out of her house, walked towards her car parked at the curb and been detoured to the black sedan double-parked in the street.

Four rather unsavory men occupied the sedan. Thugs, if truth be told. Two sat in the front, one of whom was driving, and two in the back, between whom Steinberg was sandwiched. The vehicle was luxurious, no getting around that, and the experience would have been better appreciated in different company. They did not speak to her outside of those words that had stopped her from getting into her own car: "Mr. van Dyne wishes to talk to you."

And that was it. They'd guided her to the waiting sedan and put her in it. Where they were taking her, she had no idea. Her query had been met with silence. But wherever it was, it wasn't in the city. They'd driven out of DC and were in Maryland. Rural Maryland, and that's all she knew.

They'd been driving for forty-five minutes when the driver

pulled off the paved road and onto a dirt one. After several minutes, it became clear the dirt road was a driveway to a farm, for as the car drove around a curve in the road a three-story house, a barn, and several outbuildings came into view.

In the fields, Steinberg noticed row after row of brown plants. She had no idea what they were and had no clue as to where she was. She didn't even know there were farms in Maryland.

The car pulled up to an outbuilding and came to a stop. The men got out and motioned for the congresswoman to do so as well. When she hesitated for longer than was to their liking, one of the men pointed a gun at her. No more hesitation! She left the vehicle quickly.

Two of the men walked her to the building and slid the large wood door open. Inside were two tractors. The larger of the two was a green monster. Steinberg had never seen a vehicle that huge, other than perhaps a semi. The gray and red tractor was considerably smaller.

On a large rattan chair in front of the small tractor sat an exceedingly pretty woman with long blond hair. She wore a white dress that easily reached her ankles, with long sleeves, and a high neckline. Standing next to her was a very tall and slim man. He was quite good looking, with his blond hair, beard, and mustache. He wore a black suit. A very expensive black suit.

The man began speaking and Steinberg at once recognized the voice as belonging to van Dyne. She'd met him once, a long time ago; so long ago, she'd more or less forgotten his face. But no one could forget that sneeringly commanding voice.

"Ms. Steinberg, so good of you to come."

"As if I had a choice, Mr. van Dyne."

He chuckled. "No, you didn't. At least not much of one. However, between death and a pleasant ride in the country I think you chose well. Just another of the many hundreds of annoying little decisions we must make every single day."

"We could have discussed philosophy on the phone."

Van Dyne barked a laugh. "Yes, we could have. But my intention is not to discuss philosophy. I find the subject boring. I deal with reality, not theory. Such as the reality of your failure to give me what I want with regard to Doctor Rafe Bardon and the Office of Unidentified Phenomena."

"He doesn't exist, and neither does the office."

"Yet, I say they do." He motioned with his hand, and a man stepped out of the shadows. "A chair for the congresswoman."

A chair was produced and set so it faced the wall between the two large sliding wood doors. Steinberg sat. A screen was set up, and van Dyne tapped on his tablet. In a moment, video began to play on the screen.

Van Dyne explained. "This is video footage I took myself with one of my drones of an OUP operation in a small borough in western Pennsylvania. Please watch."

And Diane Steinberg did watch. For an hour she watched the carefully edited video. When it was over, she looked at van Dyne, shifted her gaze to the pretty woman in the long, white dress, and turned back to van Dyne.

"What the hell did I just watch?"

Van Dyne, his voice quiet and unemotional, said, "You watched the Office of Unidentified Phenomena interfere with my experiment."

"What was your experiment?" Steinberg asked.

The woman spoke. "The zuvembies, Ms. Steinberg. They are my brother's experiment."

"What the hell is a zuvembie? And who are you?"

"I am Hadria van Dyne, Valdis's younger sister. Does that satisfy your curiosity about me?"

Steinberg nodded.

"What is a zuvembie, you ask?" She looked over at her brother. "What should we say, Valdis?" And without waiting for him to answer, she turned back to Steinberg. "You can think of it as anti-life. The zuvembie is alive, but it's existence has one purpose, and one purpose only. That purpose is death."

Van Dyne made a signal with his hand. Everyone except for Steinberg put on ear protection. He said, pointing, "Behold, the zuvembie!"

Steinberg followed his pointing finger. A man opened a door to what looked like a closet or a cupboard set up against the building's wall. Inside, in the darkness, was a vaguely human form. At least that's how Steinberg interpreted what she saw. From the darkness came a sweet, yet weirdly wordless melody. Just a voice vocalizing.

Darkness, as though it had poured out of that closet, enveloped the congresswoman, surrounding her as completely as the song.

After a time, Steinberg felt herself emerge from the darkness. As though she'd been underwater and had surfaced just in time to take air into her lungs and avoid drowning.

Standing outside of the closet was a horrible looking thing. At one time it might have been a teenaged woman, but now...? And Steinberg was shuffling toward the thing. In the black-taloned claws the thing had for hands was a grass hook.

Steinberg only knew what it was because she'd seen someone using one once when she was on the campaign trail and had asked about it.

The undulating melody had taken control of Steinberg's body. Her mind was screaming for her to run and she tried, but her body failed to obey. A whimper escaped her lips, but her feet shuffled on towards the hideous thing before her.

The grass hook held firmly in its right hand, the monstrosity raised the knife-like tool above its head. Steinberg knew she was going to die. This thing, this hideous caricature of a woman, this zuvembie, was going to kill her.

Without warning, she could no longer hear the melody. She felt the ear protection muffs and saw a bag put over the creature's head. The thing was shoved back into the closet and the door shut. Steinberg had stopped walking, and her body returned to her control.

She was guided back to the chair and hands none too gentle pushed her into it, removing the ear protection at the same time.

"What do you think?" Hadria van Dyne asked. "Exhilarating to face death, isn't it?"

"Now, now, Hadria. Let us not torment Ms. Steinberg. She might not appreciate our humor." Van Dyne walked in front of the congresswoman. A smile on his lips. "You have a choice, Ms. Steinberg."

Diane Steinberg looked into van Dyne's eyes. Fear, loathing, and hatred crossed her face, but it was the fear that remained.

Van Dyne leaned down, his face mere inches from hers. "You will find Doctor Bardon. You will find the Office of Unidentified Phenomena. You will tie him and his office down in a web of Congressional investigatory nonsense and you will strip his office of its financing, or close it down altogether. He must be stopped. Do you understand?"

Steinberg nodded.

Van Dyne stood upright. "Good. Because if you do not find him, no one will be able to find you."

22

COMPANY'S COMING

FROM THE SAME copse of trees that Mostyn and NicAskill had observed the Van Dyne corporate headquarters several months ago, Mostyn and his handpicked cohorts studied the building and the surrounding grounds.

The night sky was somber. Clouds had rolled in and threatened rain. The only light came from the sodium lamps surrounding the building. Somewhere up there, in the sky, Jackson floated in Bardon's Folly, the personal blimp that the OUP Research and Development wonks had converted for the agency's use. Jackson had released the drones and passed on information as it came in to him.

Jeffries did a superb job outfitting us, Mostyn thought. *We should have everything we need to pull off this mission.*

To keep in communication with each other and to protect themselves from the zuvembie's voice, should they encounter one, each team member wore a close-fitting balaclava of lightweight material that contained the communication equipment, which was computer programmed to cut out automatically any human or human-sounding voice other than those of the team members. There was a selector switch to allow person-to-person communication from someone outside the team, but that was to be used only in an emergency.

The balaclava also had a holographic information transmitter. It was connected with the OUP's computer network and provided real time information, 3-D maps, weapon targeting, and various non-visual and enhanced visual scanners.

They also had a veritable arsenal of weapons. Silenced pistols and submachine guns. Stun, smoke, fragmentation, and thermite grenades. NicAskill carried the M-88 portable lightning generator.

Their body suits contained digital devices which made them invisible to the building's security cameras and also allowed them to activate Class III xenophage protection. And Jeffries had assured Mostyn that sufficient blood had been given to the entities so they would be willing to perform.

Each team member's phone contained an array of specialty apps for additional protective measures if needed.

Mostyn was pleased. They'd had too few resources at Iram, and while van Dyne wasn't in the same league as the Great Old Ones and their minions, he was plenty dangerous. Mostyn looked at his watch. It was time to begin the operation.

He gave a hand signal indicating everyone should activate their suit and pressed the spot on the cuff to activate his own. A slightly warm feeling covered his body which told him the suit was active.

"Listen up, people. Helene will get Jones and NicAskill into the building. She will then come back for the rest of us. You two," Mostyn pointed to Jones and NicAskill, "are to take over the front security desk."

Jones gave Mostyn a thumbs up.

"Then with the help of Jackson, you two will access the

computer system and shut the building down. When you've accomplished that, you are to proceed to the main security center and neutralize it. Questions?"

Jones and NicAskill said, "No".

"The rest of us will follow when Helene returns. We will enter at the rear of the building. Once inside, we'll form two teams and find the lab making the Black Brew. Are you ready?"

A chorus of "Ready, Boss" answered Mostyn's question.

"Good. Helene, Jones, NicAskill move out."

The three dematerialized.

"Do we have any idea where the lab is located?" Baker asked, and added, "That's a mighty big building."

"No, we don't," Mostyn replied. "Once we've gotten into the computer system, we're hoping we'll find what floor the lab is on."

"And if we don't?" Dotty asked.

"Then we're to leave," Mostyn answered.

"I don't want to sound like Jones," Dotty said, "but as long as we're here aren't we going to blow up this hellhole?"

"No."

"For crying out loud, Mostyn, this is our chance to neutralize van Dyne."

"I know, Dot, but orders are orders."

Dotty shook her head. "Damn bureaucracy. I put my life on the line. The least Bardon can do is let me blow something up."

Mostyn, his gaze directed towards the Van Dyne building, said, "You know as well as I do, Dot, that things often get messy in an operation like this." He turned and looked at her. "Just saying."

A smile broke out on Dotty's face. "That they do, Mostyn. That they do."

Baker chuckled. "Glad we got that clarified."

Helene appeared.

"Everything go all right?" Mostyn asked.

"Yes, Mostyn Pierce. There was no one by the elevators, so I rematerialized them there."

"Good. Okay, Helene, do your thing."

Helene dematerialized Mostyn, Kemper, Baker, and herself. Mostyn always found being dematerialized somewhat disconcerting. He was there and yet he wasn't there. He could see, think, speak, and of course, move. However, he had no form. He was simply a cloud of disassembled atoms. He could pass through solid objects as though they weren't there. Yet they were. Seeing the inside of walls, feeling the inside of them, was a weird experience. Or passing through things like trees, or a highway, or earth. The words didn't exist to describe the experience.

And the speed at which one could move was unimaginable. While he admired the technology that one day might produce the transporter on *Star Trek*, the K'n-yanians had been using their minds to dematerialize and rematerialize objects and themselves for many millennia.

A woman sat at the desk, looking at a magazine. One look at her face told the team members she was bored. Dotty appeared next to her and administered a hypo. Within moments the guard was deeply asleep. Helene, Mostyn, and Baker rematerialized.

"Jones," Mostyn said into his headset, "how are you and NicAskill coming along?"

"Two of Jackson's drones have connected to the system.

Not sure what they're doing, but supposedly they are directly linked to our computers through the blimp."

Jackson cut in. "There's a bit of a war going on. The Van Dyne system is attempting to block the assault by the OUP computers."

"Who's winning?" Mostyn asked.

"The next forty-five seconds should tell us," Jackson replied.

Mostyn closed his eyes. Anything could happen in forty-five seconds. That was almost forever.

He opened his eyes and spoke into the headset, "Jones, any response from van Dyne's people?"

"Not yet."

"Good," Mostyn replied. "Let me know who won the duel."

"Company's coming," Baker announced, and, pointing, added, "From that corridor there."

23

THE BATTLE BEGINS

CHARGING around the corner was a massive three-headed dog, and right behind it, another.

Kemper opened fire with her silenced submachine gun. The bullets ripped into the lead dog and it kept coming.

The dog leaped into the air and Kemper vanished just before the creature landed on the spot where she'd been. Momentarily puzzled, the three heads looked around the room. Right behind it, the other monstrosity charged Baker, who activated the xenophage protection app.

The giant creature charged into Baker, knocking him down and in the process its three heads vaporized in the green aura surrounding him. It thrashed around for a few seconds and then lay still.

The first creature, spying Mostyn, started for him and vanished.

Mostyn took a deep breath and exhaled. Sprouting out of the floor in the place where the creature had vanished was its tail.

Helene and Dotty reappeared.

"What's up with that?" Dotty said. "That thing took those forty-fives as if they were spitballs."

"Apparently van Dyne's done a bit of genetic re-engineering," Mostyn replied. He turned to Baker. "You all right, Willie Lee?"

Baker waved off Mostyn's concern. "I'll live."

"Just our luck," Dotty said.

Baker's eyebrows lifted. "Sorry to disappoint you, Dotty."

"What? Oh, no, not you, Willie Lee. These monster dogs that don't die when shot."

A smile tugged at the corners of his lips, and Baker said, "Glad you clarified that."

"Okay people we have work to do," Mostyn said. "Baker, secure the guard so she stays nice and quiet. Dotty, you and Helene will go up the stairs there," Mostyn pointed to the ones he meant, "and check each floor."

"I thought we were supposed to get intel from the computer system," Dotty replied.

"Hopefully, we will," Mostyn said. "But we can't waste time. So, in the meantime, we do it the old-fashioned way. Baker and I will take the basement levels. Now go, you two, time's a wasting."

Helene and Dotty disappeared.

"Jackson, any word on the computer?" Mostyn asked.

"Their IT people have upgraded, but we're finally in. The elevators are shut down and their security cameras are now offline. Can't cut power to the building via the computers. Jones and NicAskill will have to do that manually."

"Hear that, Jones?" Mostyn said. "Neutralize their security headquarters and then take down the power."

"On it, Boss," Jones replied.

"Okay, Willie Lee, let's head for the lower levels."

"Why is it we always end up underground?"

"Good question. Maybe it has to do with where darkness dwells."

————

The security center was on the third floor. Jones and NicAskill obtained that information by accessing the internal directory on the company computer. They took the stairs to the third floor and slowly opened the door leading out onto the floor from the stairwell.

The elevator banks opened onto two corridors and the stairwell was located on one of the corridors nearby. The floor was quiet. Down the length of each corridor, on both sides, were offices and conference rooms.

"I bet the big shots have the offices on the outside walls with the windows," NicAskill said.

"You won't find me disagreeing with you," Jones replied.

The building schematic had been uploaded to the OUP computer so it was available via the holographic information transmitter in their suits.

Jones said, "Van Dyne building, third floor," and a three-dimensional image of the floor appeared before him. He spoke again, "locate security office," and part of the green outline turned red.

"See that, Nicky?" he asked.

"Yep. Got it."

The security center took up a sizable amount of space in the central office area.

"This is where we could really use Ms. Stealth," Jones said.

"That dematerializing would come in handy," NicAskill agreed.

"Isolate security office," Jones said.

The rest of the floor disappeared from the holographic image.

"It looks like these double doors lead to the front desk area," NicAskill said, pointing with her finger. "And these two doors, here, and here," she pointed to the spots on the hologram, "which are just up ahead of us, lead to the inner areas of the security center."

"Agree," Jones said, "and I bet we'll find them locked."

NicAskill nodded. "Probably." She reached into her pocket and produced a card. "That's why I took this off the guard."

"Good thinking."

"You should try it sometime, Jonesy."

"Very funny. Hologram off." The image vanished. "Let's go."

They started down the corridor when one of the doors NicAskill had identified as an entrance into the inner areas of the security center opened and two men came out. Both armed. They were talking and didn't notice Jones and NicAskill right away. When they did, it was too late. Both OUP agents fired their pistols. Four soft pffts sounded in the corridor, and the Van Dyne security people fell to the floor.

"Now we really have to hurry," Jones said.

"One of these doors, or the front desk and waiting area?" NicAskill asked.

"The front area probably has fewer people, if any, at this time of night. Be easier for us to enter."

"Sounds good."

The two agents moved down the corridor hugging the wall and stopped short of the glass wall marking the waiting area.

NicAskill brought up the holographic image of the security

center and pointed. "We can enter the security center from the double doors to the waiting area."

"But the cross corridor they open on to connects this corridor with the one on the other side of the building."

"Okay," NicAskill replied, a bit of hesitation in her voice.

"That means we'll be exposed to people or things coming to the security offices from either corridor."

"What do you propose?"

"This." Jones activated the xenophage, walked a few steps forward and turned, facing the glass wall of the waiting area. He gave his partner a thumbs up and moved forward, letting the green aura of the daemonus dissolve the glass.

The guard at the front desk jumped up and fired four rounds at Jones. The bullets vaporized upon touching the aura.

NicAskill stepped from behind Jones and fired a double tap. The guard's arms flew up, and he fell backwards. She ran to the fallen man and checked him for signs of life.

He was still breathing. She removed a patch from one of the pouches on her belt and, ripping away the wrapper, stuck it on the man's neck.

She saw Jones looking at her. "Morphine patch," she explained. "If he lives, he won't be bothering us."

Jones deactivated the xenophage. "Softy."

"Shut up, Jones. Don't you have something to blow up?"

"I do, and so do you."

NicAskill nodded and got up.

Red lights began flashing.

"Looks as though someone in the back area is calling for help," Jones said.

"Then we'd better get a wiggle on it."

And the two moved into the back areas of the security offices.

24

UP THE ANTE

IN THE COMPLEX beneath his mansion, Valdis Damien van Dyne watched the OUP operatives make their assault on his corporate headquarters and research facility.

He looked over at his sister. Hadria was watching the monitors with interest.

"We are recording this," he told her. "An unwarranted attack by the US government upon its own citizens. And we are able to do so, because we upgraded our security cameras after their last attack to counter stealth measures. "

"You will give the video to the congresswoman?"

"I will if we can use it to bring down Bardon and his Office of Unidentified Phenomena."

"We need to find out what that green halo is that they activate, and if it is something we can use."

Pointing at one of the screens, he said, "Did you catch that? Those two women simply vanished."

"Are you sure, Valdis? No one simply vanishes."

"I am very sure. And one of the women was the same woman who did the vanishing act in Oldenburg."

Hadria watched Helene and Dotty reappear. "Well, my dear brother, it looks as though we now have two things we need to obtain from Doctor Bardon."

"I agree. We need to find out how that woman is able to disappear and reappear, and we need to find out the nature of that green halo and if we can produce it ourselves."

"So, my dear brother, you might want to rethink eliminating Doctor Bardon. At least until we learn his secrets."

"You are right, Hadria. We must not be overly hasty." He studied the screens before commenting further. "The new GMO security is vastly improved. We can probably start marketing it."

The screens went dark. Van Dyne pressed a button. "Rolf, what happened?"

"They've hacked into our computer system and taken the security cameras offline. I'm switching over to the backup system as we speak."

The screens came back on and the van Dyne's once again saw the OUP operatives in action.

"Rolf, let the OUP agents have their way. We will lull them into a sense of complacency and then hit them. And hit them hard."

"Yes, Mr. van Dyne."

Hadria took her brother's hand in hers. "You are so very wicked, my love. So deliciously wicked."

———

Miriam Abramowitz lay on top of her desk considering her options as to how she was going to get into Epstein's computer. Years of practice enabled her to make the appropriate noises pretty much on autopilot until he'd climaxed.

Thank God that's over, she said to herself. She just hoped she could find what Diane Steinberg wanted so she could get the hell out of there.

He was zipping up. *God*, she thought, *doesn't even give me something to wipe up his shit.*

"Hey, Rob." She pointed. "Think you can get me a tissue."

"Sure, hon."

Hon, is it? she thought. *Okay, let's play that card.*

He handed her a tissue, she wiped, and stood up, tossing the tissue in the wastebasket.

"Say, Rob, Diane is really, really pissed."

He straightened his tie. "Yeah, probably is."

"But you can get the heat off us if you tell her about Bardon and the Office of Unidentified Phenomena."

Rob Epstein stood there looking at her. "Is this a game?"

"Game? What do you mean?"

"I mean... Never mind. Look. There is no Bardon and there is no Office of Unidentified Whatever. I've told you that and I've told Diane that."

"But she's convinced both exist. So tell her. You know, to keep the heat off us. After all you want to be with me, don't you, hon?"

"I do, but what do you mean? Keep the heat off us?"

"If Diane hauls your ass before her committee, or mine for that matter, or maybe starts a rumor or two about you having a compromising affair, well, you don't want that, do you?"

"No."

"So how about you leave your computer on and let me do some looking?"

"That is definitely—"

She took his hand and put it on her left breast. "You like that, right?"

"You know I do."

She moved his hand down between her legs. "And that?"

"Oh, yes."

"Diane can blow all this up for us. But, even though she's pissed, if I tell her I went through everything on your computer, she'll accept it that there is no Doctor Bardon and no Office of Unidentified Phenomena. And then she'll get off our backs so you can put me on mine. What do you say?"

She rubbed his hand across her so he could feel her moistness and even threw in a moan. Rob buckled.

"Okay. But be careful."

"I will." She knelt in front of him. "Are you in a real hurry to get home?"

————

A voice came over the intercom. "We have movement on the perimeter of the estate, Mr. van Dyne. Visual shows eleven men trespassing."

Van Dyne made a fist. "Release the Jersey Devils and send out the zuvembies."

25

ENTER THE DARKNESS

HELENE AND DOTTY stopped on the second floor, quickly discovered it only contained offices, disappeared from view, and moved on. The two women bypassed the third, knowing Jones and NicAskill would be at work there.

Rematerializing on the fourth floor, they spotted the giant four-armed ogre-like being at the same time it spotted them. The women disappeared and made their way to one of the two labs, leaving behind the puzzled monster.

The room was small. On the right, curving around to the back wall, were cabinets covered with a white countertop. Shelves filled the walls almost to the ceiling.

On the left was a glass wall that allowed one to look into an almost identical room on the other side. A door connected the labs.

Along the glass wall was another row of cabinets covered with a white tabletop. Several gadgets filled the space. Gadgets that even Dotty could only guess at what purpose they served.

In the middle of the room was a rectangular island with

cabinets beneath, on which were a couple of microscopes. A sink was on the near end. A row of glass shelves ran down the middle of the island.

Dotty spied a computer at the far end of the row of equipment along the glass wall. She walked to it, sat, and fired it up. With instructions from Jackson, she accessed the files to get what Van Dyne Corp was working on in Lab 4A. After a minute, Dotty concluded there was no Black Brew in the lab.

The door opened and the ogre thing entered. Helene dematerialized herself and Dotty and they passed through the door into Lab 4B.

They remained invisible, hoping to throw off the monster. It opened the door to the second lab, and, not seeing them, left.

Helene rematerialized the two of them and Dotty hurried over to the computer. She confirmed that the Black Brew was not being developed and produced on the fourth floor.

They dematerialized, made their way to the stairwell, and moved up to the fifth level.

The stairwell and the elevators opened onto a sizable open area. On one side were windows looking out over the New Jersey countryside, and on the other was a wall with a large window in the center and doors on either side. The window had curtains drawn on the inside, which blocked the view into the room.They remained invisible and walked through the wall, entering the lab. When the women were certain there was no danger, Helene rematerialized them.

Dotty turned on the lights and sat at one of the computers, while Helene looked around the lab. It was much larger than the other labs they'd seen. There were three large islands, as well as workstations along the walls. In addition, a refrigeration unit occupied a spot along the back wall.

Helene was so absorbed in looking at everything in the lab that it was only at the last moment she heard the click of nails on the tile floor. She vanished and the Cerberus monster passed through her. It stopped, and the creature's three heads sniffed the air.

The invisible Helene stood next to the creature, reached into its body, dematerialized the monster's heart, and withdrew it. The giant three-headed dog dropped dead, lying in a heap.

Helene reappeared and dropped the thing's heart next to the body. She walked to where Dotty was working at the computer, all the while looking at the beast's blood on her hand.

"Do you not think it strange, my sister, that there are not more guards around?"

"Thinking like that is going to jinx it," Dotty replied, without looking up from the computer.

"Jinx? What is 'jinx'?"

Before Dotty could answer, the door burst open. Helene and Dotty vanished as a stream of machine gun bullets cut through the air where their physical forms had been.

————

Mostyn and Baker descended to the basement level. Underground parking comprised two-thirds of the space. The remaining third was made up of storage units, the heating plant, and the emergency power generators.

"Jones, where are you?" Mostyn asked.

"Nicky and I have just destroyed the security center. We're on our way to the basement—"

"Cancel that," Mostyn interrupted. "Coordinate with Kemper and Dubreuil. Baker and I will knock out the power."

"Roger, Mostyn. Nicky and I will rendezvous with Dotty and Helene."

Mostyn brought up the hologram of the basement level. "Here is the emergency generator room and here is where the power comes into the building. We'll knock out the emergency power source first, then the main power."

Baker gave Mostyn a thumbs up.

The men walked through the supply area, past the heating plant, past where the power came into the building, and stood before the door to the emergency generator room.

Mostyn looked at Baker. "Xenophage on!"

Baker chuckled. "Always wanted to be the Human Torch, eh?"

"Sure, why not?"

Mostyn extended his hand and the green aura surrounding it made contact with the doorknob. The knob and lock vaporized. Baker pushed the door open. Mostyn entered, and a giant Cerberus creature attacked him. The heads vaporized when they touched the aura, and the beast fell dead at Mostyn's feet.

Baker heard a noise and looked behind him. "Company!" he yelled and pulled the trigger on the submachine gun.

A huge ogre with two heads and four arms stopped, absorbing the impact of the forty-five caliber bullets. When Baker ran out of ammunition, the giant monstrosity started walking towards him and Mostyn. Baker activated the xenophage. The protective shield surrounded him just as the giant thing grabbed him with its four hands, which vaporized in the glow.

The thing howled in agony. Baker plunged his arm into its

gut. The aura from the xenophage burned through skin and muscle, penetrating into the stomach. Using his arm in the manner of a knife, Baker slashed left, then right. The giant staggered backward and dropped to the floor.

A thing that resembled an enormous squid on the legs of a spider ran towards them from the opposite end of the basement.

"Good grief," Baker said, "who thinks up these things?"

"A person with a very sick mind," Mostyn answered.

The creature stopped, examined its fallen compatriot, prodding the body with a tentacle tip. When the ogre didn't respond, the new monstrosity turned its attention to the agents.

"Looks like it's trying to figure out what to do," Baker said.

"It does, doesn't it?"

The tip of one tentacle, hovering mere millimeters above the green bubble surrounding Mostyn, dipped to touch the aura. It vaporized, and the creature quickly pulled back the now slightly shorter appendage. The thing began chittering, turned around, and ran away.

"Well, I'll be damned," Baker said. "It's intelligent."

"Seems like it. Van Dyne's definitely made improvements."

"I wonder if that chittering sound was a form of speech?"

"That's where my money is going. Come on, let's disable this equipment."

Mostyn looked over the huge generator. He walked up to it and leaned against the machine. The protective bubble of the xenophage vaporized the metal like sunlight dissipating mist. He extended his arm and vaporized the cylinders.

The oil pan and filter vanished when touched by Baker. "This is almost too easy, Mostyn."

"It is, so quit jinxing it."

Mostyn stepped back, disengaged the xenophage, and looked over the huge piece of what was now scrap metal. "That ought to do it. Now, let's cut the power to this place."

Baker disengaged his protection, and the men retraced their steps to where the power lines came into the building.

"R and D just might have to rethink this use of the Class III xenophage," Baker said. "It could make a fabulous offensive weapon."

Mostyn raised his eyebrows. "It could at that, Willie Lee. Make sure to let Jeffries know."

Mostyn looked at the metal tubes housing the cables and the metal boxes covered in gauges and meters.

"A chainsaw would be nice," Baker said, "like in *Die Hard*."

Mostyn laughed.

Baker activated the Class III xenophage, extended his arm, and swiped it through the five metal tubes. The green aura cut through the tubes and wires faster than a carving knife through a spit-roasted pig.

Arcs of blue-white electricity leapt from the severed cable ends, mingled with the protective bubble, and surrounded Baker in a coruscating light show of blue, white, and green. He stood there as though transfixed, then all went dark, and he collapsed in a heap.

"Willie Lee! Are you okay?" Mostyn knelt beside him, turned on the wrist light, and felt for a pulse. He breathed a sigh of relief when he felt one. "Willie Lee, wake up." Mostyn slapped his team member's face.

"Man. What happened?" Baker said.

"You just discovered the fly in the soup. Apparently that much electricity and the xenophage don't get along. Are you okay?"

"Yeah, I think so."

Mostyn helped Baker to stand. Once on his feet, Baker tried to activate the xenophage defense, but it was gone.

"Something else to let Jeffries know about," Mostyn said, and slipped on his headlamp.

Baker did likewise, and said, "Now we've truly entered the darkness."

26

LIGHTS OUT

HELENE AND DOTTY, invisible to the four humans and the two ogre-like monsters that had entered the lab, watched as the Van Dyne security personnel surveyed the room looking for the intruders.

"Hey, Bill, over here," one of the humans said.

Dotty listened to the man who she assumed was 'Bill' utter an expletive when he saw the dead Cerberus, and then another when he saw the thing's heart on the floor next to it.

"Can you believe that?" the first man said.

"I don't want to, but I guess I have to," Bill replied.

Helene was giggling with glee.

"Pleased with yourself, aren't you?" Dotty said.

"Oh, yes, my sister. Watch this."

The invisible Helene walked up to the back of the nearest two-headed monstrosity. She reached inside its body, dematerialized its heart, and withdrew it. She reappeared, threw the heart at the man named Bill, and disappeared as the ogre crashed to the floor.

"Oh, shit! Oh, shit!" Bill exclaimed.

The other man jumped back. "Jesus Christ on a cracker. What the hell?"

The other guards came over, one of them saying, "What's going on over here?"

"Get ready, my sister."

"Wait, what—"

Helene rematerialized herself and Dotty, fired her submachine gun at the four guards and they expired in a hail of lead.

There was a roar and Helene went sprawling to the floor.

Dotty jumped forward, turned, brought up her submachine gun, and pulled the trigger. Forty-five caliber bullets slammed into the giant ogre. It staggered backwards under the impact. But when the last round in the magazine had been expended, the thing shook itself, and started towards Dotty.

"Oh shit," Dotty whispered. She ran to one of the islands, pulled the pin on a fragmentation grenade, tossed it at the lumbering creature, while taking cover.

The blast rocked the room. Dotty stayed hunkered down until stuff stopped falling and the smoke cleared. At that point she peered over the top. What was left of the fiend was lying in the aisle. She stood and walked over to it.

Below the waist was pretty much a pulpy mass. Dotty figured the concussion from the blast either killed the monster or rendered it unconscious, and then it bled to death from the wounds.

She trotted over to Helene and knelt down next to her.

"Come on, Sleeping Beauty, time to get up." She turned Helene over and slapped her cheeks.

Helene's eyes fluttered open.

"Can you hear me?" Dotty asked.

"Yes, my sister, I can hear you."

"Good. How many fingers do you see?"

"Three on your left hand and one on your right."

"Good. You'll live. Come on, we have work to do."

Then the lights went out.

———

Jones had just set off two thermite grenades in the security offices when Mostyn told him that he and NicAskill were to rendezvous with Dotty and Helene.

The complex of rooms was burning, although for how long was the question as the sprinkler system had activated.

"By the time we're done with this place," Jones said, rubbing his hands together, "van Dyne will need a new headquarters building."

"Maybe we ought to go a bit easy," NicAskill admonished. "After all, we're not on a search and destroy mission."

"Yeah, yeah. This bastard needs to be destroyed."

Jones and NicAskill made for the stairs to join Dotty and Helene. Smoke billowed from the security center, filling up the corridors. Jones got to the stairwell first and opened the door. On the other side was a giant ogre-like monster. One of its massive fists smashed Jones in the gut, sending him halfway across the corridor.

NicAskill aimed carefully and fired her pistol. The bullet penetrated the left eye of the right head. The creature's left side went limp, and the thing fell to the floor.

Dropping to the floor so her head was on the same level with the thing, NicAskill aimed and waited. The monster fired a few shots in her direction, but they were too high. The creature tried to get NicAskill in the pistol's sights and turned the left head towards her.

NicAskill squeezed the trigger and a forty-five caliber lead round nose bullet smashed through the left eye and scrambled the monster's brain.

The thing lay still.

She jumped up and ran to Jones.

"Jonesy, are you okay?"

He lay there still as death.

"Jones, talk to me." Nothing. "Jones!"

NicAskill shook him, and screamed, "Jones!"

His eyes fluttered open. "I might recover faster if you kissed me."

"You fucker! You scared the shit out of me."

Jones sat up. "That thing did pack a punch. Took me a bit to catch my breath. Probably have a bruise."

"Van Dyne should clone you."

Jones got to his feet and offered NicAskill his hand. "What's that supposed to mean?"

She took his hand and pulled herself to her feet. "Come on. We've got work to do."

The hall went dark.

"I guess Mostyn and Baker took care of the power," Jones said.

They put on their headlamps and once again made for the stairwell.

27

VAN DYNE FIGHTS BACK

VAN DYNE WATCHED the OUP operatives make a mess of his building and take apart his security force. But the one who intrigued him most was the tall woman with the alabaster skin.

"Is the fact she can disappear the only thing that attracts you about her?"

"Now, Hadria, this is no time to be jealous. You know what she would do for our plans."

"Yes, I know, Valdis. I just hope you don't get other ideas."

"I am for you. Only you. You understand that, don't you?"

"You are? You're completely and totally mine?"

"I am. I love you, Hadria. You are my life."

She kissed him. "When will you spring the trap?"

"Soon." He pressed a button. "Rolf, what of the intruders on the estate?"

"They are being taken care of."

"Good. Thank you." Van Dyne turned his attention back to the monitors. "What are they going to do next?"

The van Dynes watched one of the OUP agents activate the

green aura and cut through the power cables coming into the building.

Van Dyne smiled and said to his sister, "You see, Hadria, nothing is invincible. Even this, what shall we call it, magic, that Bardon controls? Even that has limits."

Hadria moved the virtual joystick, brought the drone in closer, and switched to infrared. "He's still alive, but it seems his green protector is gone."

"That it does. We've found a chink in Bardon's armor." Van Dyne pressed a button. "Rolf, very high voltage electricity disables that peculiar aura they generate. Which means whatever that thing is it must have a limit, a maximum capacity it can handle."

"Noted, sir."

"Use this to our advantage. Everything is expendable."

"Yes, sir."

Van Dyne released the button. "Now we will defeat Doctor Rafe Bardon."

———

On the grounds of the Van Dyne mansion, ten OUP agents took up positions to surround the house, cutting the place off from the rest of the world. Some distance away, the OUP hierophant unfolded the legs on one of the two cases he carried, and then opened the case, which housed a computer. Next to him, on the ground, was a second case.

"Mr. H to team leader, are you in position? Over."

"Team leader to Mr. H, we are in position. You may begin. Over."

"Activating algorithm now."

The hierophant typed in the command, and the computer

began running the algorithm. He waited for the prompts to appear on the screen.

"Anytime now," he muttered. "And there it is."

He opened the case at his feet, extracted a vial, and opened it. He pressed continue on the computer and poured out a small amount of the blood the vial contained.

"Team leader to Mr. H. We have hostiles. Repeat. We have hostiles. Can you speed things up?"

"Negative, team leader. Another two-and-a-half minutes."

He heard an expletive in reply.

"I'm not a bloody miracle worker."

His attention focused on the computer screen, he failed to notice the flying figure above him. Not until the protective bubble sprang up around him did the hierophant realize that he was also under attack.

"Damn it." Through the haze he saw the strange creatures surrounding him.

A prompt appeared on the screen and as the hierophant reached for the second vial, over a dozen Jersey Devils hit the green aura at the same time. They vaporized, and the aura disappeared.

Two Devils swooped in. The hierophant pressed the red destruct button on the case just before the Devils picked him up and carried him off into the night sky.

———

Doctor Rafe Bardon followed the unfolding drama at the Van Dyne corporation headquarters building and at the Van Dyne mansion. Circling each, at an altitude of twenty thousand feet, was a large military drone converted for OUP operations.

He was losing the battle at the mansion. And he didn't like

it. Not one bit. Next to him was his secretary and personal assistant, Evelyn.

"If you wait much longer, Doctor Bardon, there won't be anything left to salvage."

"Yes, Evelyn, you're right. Mr. Van Dyne has proven to be quite adaptive and resilient." He sighed. "Very well. Let's prepare for battle."

28

VIPER'S DEN

DOTTY FISHED her headlamp out of a pouch on her belt and put it on. "Mostyn, you there?"

"I'm here, Dotty."

"How the hell am I supposed to check the computer files if there's no power?"

Jackson's voice cut in. "The bots crawling through the Van Dyne computer files aren't finding anything related to zuvembies, or any other secret projects. They either have that stuff on a separate server we don't know about, or it's on paper, or tablets, or something not connected to any server."

"There's your answer, Dot," Mostyn said. "My guess is the information is on tablets not connected to the server, or on paper. That way the info can't be hacked."

"Makes sense, Mostyn," Jackson said.

Grudgingly Dotty agreed. She turned to Helene. "Come on. We have to look for records not on a computer."

"Do you mean books?" Helene asked.

"Probably sheets of paper in folders."

"Where would we find these folders?"

"Good question. Desk drawers, or filing cabinets."

"What is a filing cabinet?"

"Are you for real?"

"Yes. I am real."

Dotty bowed her head and shook it. With hands on hips, she lifted her head and slowly panned the room. "There, in that corner, that's a filing cabinet. Come on."

The two women walked over to the cabinet.

"Of course it has to be locked." Dotty pulled out her pistol.

"No, my sister." Helene pointed. "Is this brass-colored object the lock?"

"Yes."

"Watch."

Dotty watched as Helene touched the lock, and it vanished.

"God. I wish I could do that."

"Doctor Bardon tells me he thinks my ability to dematerialize is a matter of mathematics and algorithms. We K'nyanians can disassemble our molecular structure, yet keep it cohesive enough so we do not lose our identity, and then reassemble our bodies at will."

"Do you learn this ability?"

"We learn how to use this ability." Helene paused and then continued. "You are born with the ability to speak. But unless you are taught speech, you cannot speak."

Dotty nodded. "I understand. What does mathematics and algorithms have to do with it?"

"I do not know. He says the brain is an organic computer, and it functions mathematically according to the algorithms directing it."

Dotty's face was screwed up in thought.

Helene continued. "Doctor Bardon says magic is simply

science we don't understand. Magic is a set of algorithms. Musical incantations are mathematical algorithms, which open doors if all the conditions are met."

Dotty laughed. "It's all above my pay grade. Let's check out the contents of this cabinet."

"Doctor Bardon is very intelligent. Sometimes I believe he might be superior to the scholars of K'n-yan."

"Seriously?"

"Yes, my sister."

"Imagine that." Dotty pulled open a drawer and rifled through the contents of the folders. She did the same for the other three drawers. When she'd gone through all the folders, she declared there was nothing to be had in the cabinet about zuvembies.

"Now that you know what to do, let's go through all the desk and table drawers."

"That will take a long time, my sister."

"Not if you do it quickly."

"Hey, Kemper." Dotty wrinkled her nose at the sound of Jones's voice.

"I'm here, Jones. What do you want?"

"Where are you? Nicky and I are supposed to help you."

"Fifth floor lab. But we're almost done here. Meet us on six."

"Roger. See you soon."

Dotty shook her head, and muttered, "That's all I need."

———

Bringing up the 3-D holographic layout of the basement level, Mostyn found the door for the stairs to the sub-basement. He and Baker made their way to the door.

"It is pitch black in here," Baker said. "Without a light, we'd never get out of this place."

"It is dark."

"Dark doesn't even describe it, Mostyn."

"Okay, here's the door. Be prepared."

Mostyn turned the knob and pushed the door open. The putrid odor hit him like a sledgehammer, and a millisecond later recognition hit his brain. He jumped back and let the door close.

"What is it?" Baker asked.

"Snake. A giant snake just waiting for us to walk into its open mouth."

Baker removed a fragmentation grenade. "Open the door again, Boss. Let's give this thing a surprise."

Mostyn laughed. "Okay." He took a deep breath and exhaled, calming his nerves and putting out of his mind the time one of van Dyne's giant snakes had swallowed him whole. He took another deep breath and exhaled.

Baker pulled the pin on the grenade. "Ready when you are."

Mostyn nodded, turned the knob, gave the door a big push, and stepped back along the wall.

The door swung open, Baker tossed the grenade into the thing's gaping and waiting mouth, and took cover along the wall.

The door swung closed and there was a muffled boom.

Mostyn waited a few seconds, and once again opened the door. The giant serpent lay there, smoke curling out of its nose.

The men maneuvered around the enormous head, their headlamps illuminating the stairwell.

"Look at this thing," Baker said. "It has to be, what, forty or fifty feet long?"

"I'd say that. And given its girth, the thing probably weighs over a ton."

"You're lucky to be alive."

"Thanks to Dotty's quick thinking," Mostyn said, recalling that cave in Appalachia. "Looks as though the only way down is by crawling over this thing."

Baker shrugged. "Into the viper's den."

29

THE OUP TAKES A BEATING

"WHAT I DON'T GET," Jones said, "is why we haven't met with a full-scale counterattack."

NicAskill shrugged. "Maybe there's nothing here of major importance. Maybe he moved the top secret stuff out of here after Mostyn's and my visit."

"Probably did. Which means we're on nothing but a wild goose chase."

"Could be, Jonesy, could be."

"What I also don't get is why I gave up a good job with the Bureau to work here. Sure, the pay's better... I just don't know why I let Bardon talk me into it."

"You know he might not have talked you into it."

"What do you mean?"

"It might be he let a little magic do the talkin'."

"Aw, shit. You think so?"

NicAskill gave Jones a peck on the lips. "Uh-huh."

Jones smiled. "On the other hand, it could be the benefits package. The OUP has a mighty good benefits package." He paused for a moment, then nodded. "Yep, definitely the benefits."

"Perhaps." She gave him another peck on the lips. "C'mon. We have work to do."

"Right."

The two OUP agents took the stairs up to the sixth floor. Outside the door, Jackson's voice sounded in their ears.

"Listen up. There's a lot of activity on floors ten through fifteen. I'm also picking up activity in sub-basement levels three and four. We also have a complication. Van Dyne has launched drone hunters. They are highly efficient and we're losing the drone war. I'm recalling the survivors as I speak. Which means I'll have little—"

Jackson's voice was cut off by a muffled explosion.

————

Mostyn and Baker had just entered the first sub-basement level when Jackson started speaking. When his transmission was cut off, Mostyn shook his head.

"Looks as though things are heating up all around us and we're going to be flying blind. I hope Jackson is okay."

"Yeah. Where the hell does van Dyne get this stuff?"

"He's rich, Willie Lee."

"Tell me about it. You think we should abort?"

"Not yet. If van Dyne infects a major metro area with his Black Brew, we'll have more problems than we're encountering here."

"You're right. Let's find the stuff or check this place off the list."

Mostyn took a flashlight out of his pack. He turned it on and illuminated what was in front of them. Across from where they were standing were elevator doors. To their right, a wall. To their left, a wall with a door in the center.

"Left my badge at home," Baker said. He leveled his pistol at the pass card receiver and fired. The box disintegrated under the impact of the bullet. He took hold of the doorknob and pushed the door open.

In front of him stood a zuvembie. Its lips were shaped as though it were whistling. And it probably was. But Baker and Mostyn couldn't hear the music.

Baker fired his pistol. The creature toppled over backwards from the impact of the bullet, spasmed three times, and lay still.

"Listen up, everyone," Mostyn said. "Have encountered a zuvembie on sub-basement level one. I doubt this will be the only one. Baker and I will investigate. We may have found where the Black Brew is being made."

"We hear you, Mostyn," Dotty said.

"Roger that," Jones added.

The door from the stairwell opened, and a grenade bounced into the room. Baker and Mostyn dived through the doorway where the zuvembie had been standing and the grenade exploded.

———

Hadria Clovinia van Dyne watched the transmission of the battle being waged around the mansion with a smile on her face. One of the OUP agents had been hypnotized by a zuvembie and the creature had stabbed the man in the heart. She watched the creature direct the corpse to attack one of its teammates. The team member frantically fired her weapon at the corpse until it put a bullet between her eyes.

The zuvembie then released the corpse, and it fell to the ground.

Valdis Damien van Dyne was watching the duel between his drone and the OUP drone, which dived, turned, and shot a stream of lead into his Turkish machine.

He watched as his drone returned fire until the OUP machine disappeared in a bright orange fireball.

With a smile on his lips, he pressed a button. "Rolf, eliminate the intruders at headquarters."

"Yes, sir."

Van Dyne released the button and put his arm around his sister. "I do believe, my dear Hadria, the victory is ours."

————

Mostyn shook his head. Thank God for the ear protectors, although he felt bruised from the concussion of the blast. He looked around the room, following the flashlight and headlamp beams. Baker got to his feet, adding his headlamp beam in an attempt to penetrate the darkness. Looking back at them were dozens of pairs of eyes.

"You know, Mostyn, I think we jumped straight into the fire."

"Heads up everyone," Mostyn said. "Sub-basement level one. On the double. Willie Lee and I just found Ali Baba's treasure room."

————

Helene dematerialized Dotty, Jones, NicAskill, and herself. In short order, they reappeared next to Mostyn and Baker, who'd taken cover behind a large island with drawers, cupboards, and countertop with a sink. They were shooting at pairs of eyes shining in the headlamp beams.

"We took out a couple of lurkers in the stairwell, Boss," Jones said, and added, "Why not use grenades on them?"

"I don't want to destroy the place before finding the Black Brew," Mostyn replied.

"Okay," Jones said. "How about Nicky, Ms. Stealth, and I take care of it?"

Mostyn looked at Jones. "What do you propose?"

Jones activated the xenophage defense. "Hot knife through butter."

Mostyn nodded. "Oldenburg. Okay. Have at it you three."

NicAskill activated her xenophage defense, and Helene disappeared.

Dotty took a larger flashlight out of her pack, and Baker did as well. With their headlamps, the flashlights and the green auras, there was enough light to see most areas of the room.

The zuvembies began backing up before Jones and NicAskill. Helene would suddenly appear, shoot a creature, and then vanish.

There were several dead zuvembies, victims of Mostyn and Baker, and the number of bodies began growing due to Helene.

The no longer human beings had fallen back to the rear wall of the lab. There was nowhere else for them to go.

With their mouths open — Mostyn assumed they were screaming — they rushed Jones and NicAskill. Several vaporized in the green auras. Those that made it past the OUP agents were cut down with the lead bullets fired by Mostyn, Baker, and Dotty.

In a matter of moments, it was over. The floor of the lab was littered with the dead monsters.

"Okay, people, find the Black Brew," Mostyn ordered. "Helene, stand guard."

"Yes, Mostyn Pierce." She went to the door and vanished.

The rest of the team members began searching through drawers, cupboards, and filing cabinets. It was Baker who found the safe in a dark corner.

Mostyn looked at the big, solid, steel box. "There's no way we're getting that open anytime soon."

The word "company" appeared in the minds of the team members, followed by the sound of gunfire. Coming through the doorway, or attempting to, were hideous things. A human torso grafted onto the body of a giant millipede, with an octopus for a head.

Helene killed one and vanished before a tentacle was able to wrap itself around her neck.

"NicAskill, the M-88!" Mostyn yelled. He opened fire with his submachine gun. Jones and Kemper followed suit. The monstrosities fired back, with machine pistols in each hand.

NicAskill, with Baker's help, got the M-88 Portable Lighting Generator assembled. She flipped the switch, the weapon powered up, and she pointed it at the doorway.

Mostyn sent a telepathic message to Helene to take cover, and then he gave NicAskill the order to fire.

She pulled the trigger. There was the brilliant flash of a thousand suns, and a wall-shattering sonic boom.

30

THE TABLES TURN

Van Dyne watched, courtesy of a tiny drone, as Mostyn and his team eliminated the zuvembies. He also saw them discover the safe.

"Those meddlers have found it," he said, gritting his teeth.

"Don't worry, my love," Hadria said, "we have a copy of the formula safe and secure."

"Nevertheless, if they destroy the lab, we will be delayed. Significantly delayed."

Van Dyne and his sister watched Helene destroy one of the Van Dyne security guards. "We need to find out her secret," he said to his sister.

Before she could reply there was a blinding flash and the screen went dark.

Van Dyne pressed a button. "Rolf, what's going on at the headquarters building?"

"Some manner of super weapon, Mr. van Dyne. I think it's what they used before. Take a look at this, sir. We might have a bigger problem."

In a moment a video feed appeared on a screen. Van Dyne

and Hadria saw the swirling blackness in the night sky. A blackness that was darker than the night. A blackness that was moving towards the Van Dyne mansion.

"What is that, Valdis?"

"I don't know, my love."

The coruscating darkness stopped and slowly a face emerged.

Van Dyne watched it form out of the swirling and twisting darkness; and when it was complete, he gasped.

"What is it, Valdis?"

"We must go. Now."

"Valdis?"

"No time to explain, Hadria. We have to leave."

Hadria took one last look at the video feed. Her eyes grew wide, and she sucked in her breath. She was looking at the face of Doctor Rafe Bardon.

———

Mostyn smelled a cascade of odors. Burnt paint and concrete. Torched metal. Electrically charged air. Burnt flesh.

The wall and door were gone, and the concrete of the landing area was riddled with cracks. Part of the ceiling had collapsed, and the floor was covered with shattered glass.

"Helene!" Mostyn called out.

She appeared next to him. "I am here Mostyn Pierce."

"Can you tell me what is inside the safe?"

"Yes, Mostyn Pierce."

"Have at it."

Helene vanished and in a few moments reappeared. "There are papers and a bottle inside. Do you want them?"

"Yes."

Helene disappeared again, and this time the safe did as well. After a few moments, she and the safe reappeared. Helene was holding a bottle in one hand and papers and several notebooks in the other. The bottle was labeled with a number.

Mostyn looked at the papers and thumbed through the books. "These are notes on the Black Brew experiment." He took the bottle from Helene. "And this must be the Black Brew."

Dotty said, "We need to take these with us."

"We'll take the notes," Mostyn replied. He set the bottle on top of the safe. "The Black Brew we'll destroy."

He turned to NicAskill. "I'll take the M-88," Mostyn said. "Jones, get everyone out."

"Boss…"

"Just do it, Jones. I'll be right behind you."

Dotty came up to Mostyn, kissed his cheek, and told him to not be a hero.

Helene kissed Mostyn on the other cheek and told him to be careful.

Mostyn watched his team leave, and when they were gone, he walked out to the landing area by the stairwell and elevators. He pointed the M-88 at the safe and pulled the trigger.

———

Van Dyne and Hadria made their way to a door. He opened it with his pass card, and the two got into a small vehicle. Van Dyne pressed a button and the electric motor came to life. He pressed another button and in moments the car was shooting down a tunnel that would take them far away from the mansion.

31

TENTACLES

SUB-BASEMENT LEVEL ONE looked like a cyclone had hit it. The walls were fractured and part of the ceiling had fallen.

They won't be using this lab for a while, Mostyn thought.

He turned to the stairwell. In the demolished doorway stood a... Mostyn didn't know what it was. It looked like a robot. Like something out of *Robocop*. The thing pointed a gun at Mostyn, who hit the ground. He felt the bullet whiz over his head.

Mostyn rolled, and a bullet hit the concrete where he'd been lying. Another bullet grazed his shoulder, and he gritted his teeth from the burning pain.

The M-88 lay where he'd dropped it when he dove to avoid the first bullet. The thing took aim. Mostyn rolled, cried out from the shoulder pain, and retrieved a grenade.

The metal man turned. The laser from the pistol formed a dot on Mostyn's forehead. Mostyn rolled again, feeling a chunk of concrete dig into his back, and tossed the grenade.

The robot fired, and the grenade exploded.

———

Jones, NicAskill, Baker, Dotty, and Helene made their way up to the main basement level.

"We can go out through the garage doors," Jones said.

Dotty reminded him there was no power.

"Don't need it," Jones replied. "We have Ms. Stealth."

The team members ran to the garage doors. Helene dematerialized the group, and they walked through the doors.

———

Mostyn shook his head. There was a whirring sound as of gears and servo motors at work. Mostyn turned his head and saw the robot man.

The legs were mangled, and Mostyn could see flesh underneath the metal. *A cyborg,* he said to himself, *what hasn't Van Dyne thought of?*

He got to his feet and walked over to the cyborg. The thing had dropped its pistol in the blast and was flailing its arms.

Mostyn retrieved the M-88, and left the floor, climbing the stairs to the main basement level.

He sent his thoughts to Helene. *Are you out of the building?*

Yes, Mostyn Pierce, came the reply

Good. Get as far away as you can.

He ran towards the emergency generator room, pulling a thermite grenade from his belt. "Time to see what a little fire and diesel fuel will do," he said out loud.

———

Rolf watched the face form. "Do you see it, Mr. van Dyne?" When there was no response, Rolf realized his boss had fled, and decided that was the best course of action.

Out of the mouth of the face came dozens of tentacles. Tentacles made out of the inky blackness of space. The tentacles searched out every living entity on the estate and pulled them, struggling and screaming, into the maw of the face.

Rolf ran for his car and was almost to the garage, when one of those tentacles wrapped itself around his waist and lifted him, screaming, off his feet.

EPILOGUE

DOCTOR BARDON LIT HIS PIPE. Mostyn watched his boss circle the match around the bowl and puff on the pipe until he had an even burn on the tobacco.

To Mostyn, the round little Englishman looked as though he should be in front of a classroom somewhere, instead of directing what was perhaps the most secret organization on the planet.

He also thought it strange that Bardon had taken five days to have his recap of the operation meeting.

Pipe going to his satisfaction, Bardon turned his attention to Mostyn.

"Well, Pierce, my boy, Valdis Damian van Dyne has proven to be a resourceful opponent."

"Yes, sir, he has."

"Although that was good thinking on your part to demolish the internal building supports. From what I understand, the corporation has temporarily moved its headquarters to New York until the assessment comes in if the New Jersey building is salvageable."

"Thank you, sir. If I may ask, what happened at the mansion?"

"Again, van Dyne was more resourceful than I gave him credit. But we eventually got the upper hand, and a second team moved in and eliminated the underground facility. He has a lovely home."

"You didn't destroy the house?"

"Oh, no, Pierce, my boy. I wouldn't deprive a man of his castle. He simply won't be able to conduct business from there for quite some time."

Bardon puffed on his pipe before continuing. "And we shouldn't have any problems from the congresswoman, either. At least for a while. It took a bit of doing but we were able to alter selectively the memories of Ms. Abramowitz and Mr. Epstein, as well. It's amazing what a pathogoth can do."

"Jackson, sir, will he be returning to duty?"

"Oh, yes. Just minor scratches. The missile missed the gondola and detonated in the envelope. Mr. Jackson parachuted to safety."

"That's good to hear. Uh, sir, I've been meaning to ask about Doctor Heber."

"What about him?"

"He seems to have something against Helene."

"Does he, now? Hm, we'll keep an eye on him."

"Thank you, sir. Any word on van Dyne?"

"Not yet. It seems he's gone to ground. But we'll find him. He won't elude us for long."

"What about Oldenburg?"

"That was a most unfortunate affair. We rounded up what we think were all of the zuvembies, save for one. Although, we did have some competition from a team that we think was trying to rescue them." He puffed on his pipe. "I doubt that one creature will elude us for long. The PR department is handling the situation. A story about toxic waste in a landfill, or some such, I believe."

Bardon set his pipe down. "A superb job, Pierce, thank you. Enjoy your convalescence. About three weeks, I believe it is."

"Yes, sir."

Bardon stood and extended his hand. Mostyn stood and shook hands with his boss.

"Enjoy your rest, Pierce."

"I will, Doctor Bardon."

When Mostyn had departed, Bardon walked to the sideboard and poured himself a glass of vintage port. He looked at the statues of Cthulhu and Shub-Niggurath that were on either end of the piece of furniture.

He raised his glass. "You two and Helene are my souvenirs from K'n-yan, and of you three Helene is the most valuable. I will protect her with my life."

The OUP director returned to his desk and relit his pipe. He puffed on it for a while before summoning Evelyn, his secretary.

"Yes, Doctor Bardon?"

"I'd like the original vetting report on Doctor Carter Heber."

———

Several miles away on a highway in Virginia, Doctor Carter Heber's phone rang. The caller ID told him the call was from his partner, Doctor Gisella Finseth.

"Hi, Sweetheart!"

"Hello, Doctor Heber, my name is Valdis Damien van Dyne."

"W-What? Where's—?"

"Nothing has happened to your friend. I'm just borrowing her phone ID so we can speak."

"What do you want?"

"There's a woman in whom we both have an interest. Let's meet and talk. I'm sure you'll find my proposal to be most advantageous."

A WORD FROM CW

I hope you enjoyed *Van Dyne's Zuvembies*.

If you did, please leave a review where you bought the book and on your favorite social media sites. Your review is like word of mouth advertising. And it is pure gold.

Enter my World

Enter my world. A world of terror on a cosmic scale. Just click, tap, or scan the QR code below.

Fear is the most primal of human emotions. And fear of the unknown is the most terrifying of all fears.

If you are new to the Pierce Mostyn Paranormal Investigations series, then *Van Dyne's Zuvembies* is an excellent entry point into the series and into my world.

In addition to my Pierce Mostyn Paranormal Investigations books, I've written short stories set in the world of the macabre and arcane. Many of which are only available to folks on my mailing list.

So just click, tap, or scan the QR code to enter my world of terror and the macabre. You will get a free copy of *The Feeder* and you'll get my monthly email of news and curated contact. Terror awaits!

CONTINUE THE ADVENTURE!

The paranormal investigations of Pierce Mostyn continue in *In the Shadow of the Mountains of Madness*. When death's your only option.

Pierce Mostyn and his team are sent to Antarctica to find out what destroyed the Vostok Research Station. What they find doesn't bode well for humanity.

And to find out if humanity can be saved, Mostyn and his team must bore through the ice cap to reach the sub-glacial Gamburtsev Mountains — the infamous Mountains of Madness.

What Mostyn and his team discovers is a terror that may very well destroy all life on earth. Will Mostyn and his team be able to escape the horror and get back in time so countermeasures can be taken?

In the Shadow of the Mountains of Madness is the eighth book in CW Hawes's Pierce Mostyn Paranormal Investigations series.

If you love weird fiction, horror, monsters, humor, thrilling action, and the Cthulhu Mythos, get in on Pierce Mostyn's adventure today — if you dare!

In the Shadow of the Mountains of Madness is available at your favorite online store. Check it out! Click, tap, or scan the QR code.

BOOKS BY CW HAWES

CW is a multi-genre author.

The books below are portals to his many exciting worlds. And no AI was used in the writing of these books. Books by a human for a human.

Pierce Mostyn Paranormal Investigations

The X-Files meets Cthulhu. Pierce Mostyn does battle with inter-dimensional monsters bent on the destruction of humanity.

Nightmare in Agate Bay
Stairway to Hell
Terror in the Shadows
Van Dyne's Vampires
The Medusa Ritual
Demons in the Dunes
Van Dyne's Zuvembies
In the Shadow of the Mountains of Madness

Justinia Wright Private Investigator Mysteries

Justinia Wright is the PI with panache. These slow burn mysteries, written in homage to Rex Stout's Nero Wolfe, are sure to satisfy your craving for intriguing puzzles, quirky characters, and wise-cracking humor.

Vampire House and Other Early Cases of Justinia Wright, PI
Festival of Death
Trio in Death-Sharp Minor
But Jesus Never Wept
The Conspiracy Game
A Nest of Spies
When Friends Must Die
Death Makes a House Call
To Right a Wrong
The Nine Deadly Dolls
Ripples on the Pond
Christmas with the Wrights
Minneapolis's Finest
Jack in the Box
Sauerkraut Days
Justinia Wright Private Investigator Omnibus Edition

Magnolia Bluff Crime Chronicles

Tense slow burn mysteries set in our favorite town in the Texas Hill Country.

Death Wears a Crimson Hat
Ten Million Ways to Die
Who Mourns Elektra?
Death by Moonlight

The Rocheport Saga

A post-apocalyptic adventure series in the style of cozy catastrophes such as *Earth Abides* and *Day of the Triffids*. Join Bill Arthur as he strives to build a new and better world on the ashes of the old.

The Morning Star
The Shining City
The Divided City
The Troubled City
By Leaps and Bounds
Freedom's Freehold
Take to the Sky

Decopunk

Alternative history adventures in a world where World War II never happened and swing is still king.

From the Files of Lady Dru Drummond
The Moscow Affair
The Golden Fleece Affair

Rand Hart Adventures
Rand Hart and the Pajama Putsch

Tales of the Macabre

For the horror lover in you.
Do One Thing For Me
Metamorphosis
What the Next Day Brings

Ancient History

Anthologies

Enjoy CW's stories in these short story collections.

The Phantom Games
Beyond the Sea
Overmorrow
Arachnapocalypse! The Anthology
Once Upon a WolfPack

Available at your favorite online retailer. Just click, tap, or scan the QR code to be taken to My Books page and the link to your favorite online retailer.

ABOUT CW HAWES

CW Hawes has written over 50 novels and shorter works of fiction. He was also an award-winning poet and had over 200 poems appear in ezines and and print.

He is a founding member of the Underground Authors and was the impetus for the highly successful Magnolia Bluff Crime Chronicles series.

After 35 years of working in county government, he retired at the beginning of 2015 and began a second career as a fiction-eer. Perhaps some of the horrors Pierce Mostyn faces can be traced to his creator's own experiences in county government and beyond. Perhaps.

CW lives in Southern California. He enjoys reading, writing, chess and other board games, his daily morning walk, and contemplating the meaning of life while smoking his pipe. He also hasn't met a doughnut or a pizza he doesn't like, is something of a tea snob, and rocks out to Handel and Vaughan Williams.

You can get curated content and the occasional free story when you join his mailing list, and you can reach him at his website, on X, and also Facebook.

To join his mailing list, click, tap, or scan the QR code:

To visit him on his website, click, tap, or scan the QR code:

To visit him on X, click, tap, or scan the QR code:

To visit him on Facebook, click, tap, or scan the QR code: